ROXBORO BR
Tel. 4

D0264956

WITHDRAWN FROM STOCK

Limerick City Library

3 0002 00110569 1

Ride a Pale Horse

Alerting the garrison at the Sheriff's House

Tom McCaughren

RIDE A PALE HORSE

Illustrated by Terry Myler

ANVIL BOOKS

First published 1998 by
Anvil Books
45 Palmerston Road, Dublin 6

© Text Tom McCaughren 1998
© Illustrations: Anvil Books

All rights reserved. No part of this publication
may be reproduced, stored in a retrieval system,
or transmitted in any form or by any means,
electronic, mechanical, photocopying, recording
or otherwise, without the prior permission
of the publishers.

ISBN 1 901737 08 X

CITY OF LIMERICK
PUBLIC LIBRARY

Origination Computertype Ltd
Printing Colour Books Ltd
Cover: The Battle of Vinegar Hill by Terry Myler,
based on various contemporary drawings

Contents

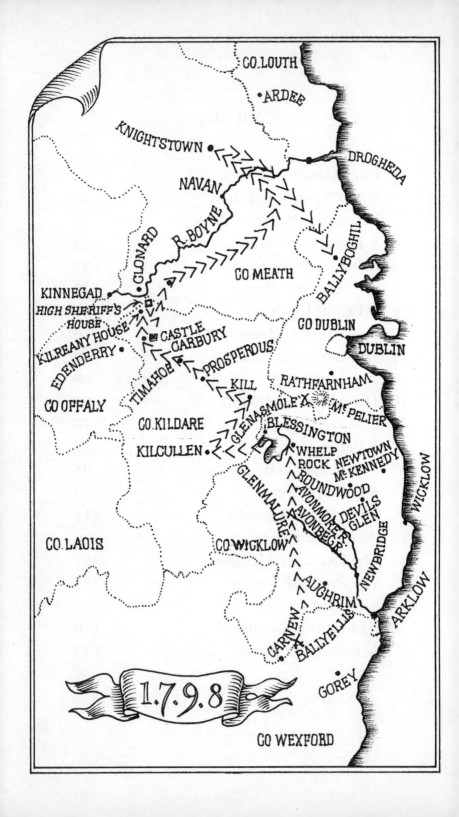

Illustrations

The Sheriff's House
at Clonard

VERITAS VIA VITAE

THE MILL

MILL RACE

DUBLIN – CLONARD – KINNEGAD →

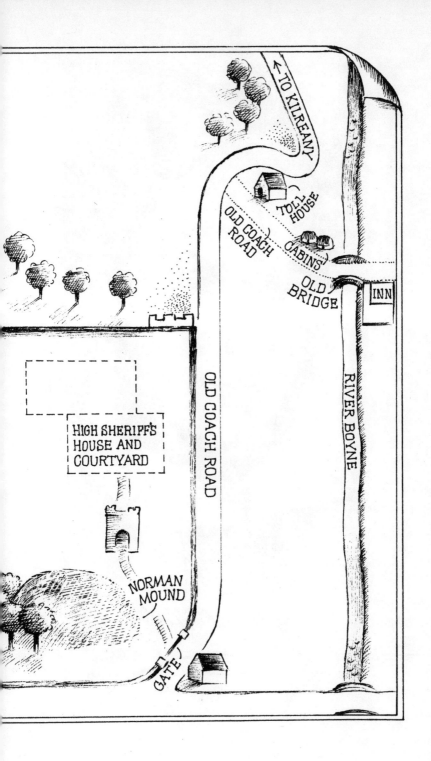

Joseph Holt

Introduction

I first became interested in General Joseph Holt when I was doing research for my first book on the Rebellion of 1798, *In Search of the Liberty Tree*. He had not been given a high profile in the history books, but I discovered that he was one of the most colourful leaders of the Rebellion. Operating in the Wicklow mountains, he was involved in many daring exploits. However, it was the plan to attack the stronghold of the High Sheriff of Kildare that led to his most exciting adventure.

Although a work of fiction, *Ride a Pale Horse* is based on actual events. While *In Search of the Liberty Tree* is told through the experiences of a boy whose family, in County Antrim, is opposed to the Rebellion, this story centres largely on the fortunes of a County Wicklow boy whose family actively supports it.

The Wicklow boy is mentioned only once in General Holt's memoirs. We aren't even told his first name, but I have assumed that he was called after his father, Tom Howlett, who was a miller in Newbridge, now the village of Avoca. As the story unfolds, young Tom Howlett is appointed Holt's *aide-de-camp* and witnesses the attack on the Sheriff's House at first hand.

It might seem somewhat fanciful so suggest that an eleven-year-old boy would be given such a position, but I have merged Tom's character with that of another, unidentified, boy who had just that experience. In later years he recounted that he had been captured by Holt's men while being escorted by the military to his uncle's house in County Wexford. Threatened with death by some of his captors, he was saved by one of the rebels who brought him before Holt. The rebel leader immediately placed the boy under his protection, made him his *aide-de-camp* and presented him with a pair of 'very nice' brass pistols.

'I continued some weeks with the rebel army,' the boy recalled, 'and was witness to several extraordinary instances of General Holt's bravery and humanity, as well as of his determined character.'

Through the eyes of another boy, the fourteen-year-old son of Lieutenant Thomas Tyrell, the High Sheriff of Kildare, we get a fascinating picture of what it was like when, besieged by thousands or rebels, the Sheriff, his family and a small garrison put up a spirited defence in a battle that proves to be a turning-point in the rebellion.

The subsequent dispersal of the rebel army, the dangerous trek home through Dublin, and the scary stopover at the Enchanted House, are based on Holt's memoirs and other historical sources. At the time of these events, Holt, in his own words, had assumed the rank of colonel. It wasn't until he returned to Wicklow that he held the more senior rank of general. He had then become commander-in-chief of the rebels, the last person to hold that position.

Tom McCaughren
1998

1

Good News – and Bad

Leaning back in the big leather chair, Tom Howlett let the evening sun shine on his face with the balmy warmth of summer. Through the half-open window of his father's study came the sound of the Avoca River as it gurgled its way past the nearby village of Newbridge, and the swish of the water-wheel as it turned beside the mill. However, these were sounds he had heard since the day he was born and he was barely aware of them.

Being the son of a miller, Tom was one of the few boys in the Avoca valley receiving an education and what he did hear was the boisterous shouts of other boys at play. Education, he knew, was a privilege the others had been denied, but how he wished he could be with them. Returning to his homework he waited for the sounds that would tell him the day's work was done. First there would be the gradual slowing down of the water-wheel, then his father would come in. A little later he would hear the door-latch being lifted again and, with the customary 'God save all here,' the first of the neighbours would arrive for their nightly chat.

Usually it was only at night, when the work of the mill was done and Tom's father was smoking his long clay pipe, that matters relating to the Rebellion were discussed. Even then they were only spoken of in undertones, as if to speak of them any louder might be to betray a confidence. By that time, Tom would be continuing his studies beneath the light of the kitchen lamp and would lift his head from his books now and then to listen.

From what was said on these occasions, Tom knew that things were not going well for those who, like his father, supported the Rebellion. The news that the forces of the United Irishmen had been defeated at the battle of

Vinegar Hill in June had been received with dismay. As far as he could gather, it had been a decisive battle, maybe even the turning-point in the Rebellion. Following their defeat, big numbers of rebels had retreated from Wexford to join their comrades in Wicklow. There they had continued to do battle with Government forces, but without much success. Then, word had filtered through that a number of their leaders had been hanged in Wexford town, while victorious regiments, especially the yeomen, had wreaked a terrible vengeance on the local population.

However, as June turned to July, word came of a victory for the rebels. According to people who called at the mill, Colonel Joseph Holt had set up an ambush on a road at Ballyellis, near Carnew, on the Wicklow-Wexford border. Then he had lured a contingent of the King's cavalry into a trap. They included members of a Welsh regiment called the Ancient Britons, for whom the local population had a particular dislike.

'From what I hear,' said Mr Howlett, 'Colonel Joe got some of his men to fire at the cavalry and then retreat, as if they were in panic. The cavalry charged after them, but when they rounded a bend they found the road blocked by horses and carts. Joe had placed some of his musketmen behind the carts and when they opened fire the cavalry tried to retreat. But they were cut off by the rest of the musketmen who had closed in behind them.'

'How come the cavalry didn't escape through the fields?' asked a neighbour.

'Because Colonel Joe had chosen his ground well,' said Mr Howlett. 'On each side of the road there were deep ditches and heavy thorn hedges that the horses couldn't get through. But Joe had hidden a thousand pikemen behind the hedges and had them make secret holes in the thorn so that they could get through. They closed in and it was all over in less than twenty minutes.'

'How many were killed?' asked another neighbour.

Mr Howlett puffed at his pipe and told him, 'The figure I heard was three hundred and seventy.'

'Altogether?'

'No, of the King's troops.'

'As many as that?'

'That's what I hear,' said Mr Howlett.

'It was a great victory,' said another man with a shake of his head. 'A great victory.'

'A feather in the cap for Colonel Joe,' said the man beside him. 'And the Ancient Britons had it coming to them.'

Mrs Howlett got up and busied herself at the table, an indication that she didn't like to hear of such slaughter, even if some of the slain were members of the Ancient Britons. She also knew that revenge would surely follow and that the ordinary people were likely to suffer.

'But, of course,' added Mr Howlett, sensing his wife's discomfort, 'the military say they only lost about forty or fifty.'

A man who was nursing a small glass of whiskey on his knee inquired, 'And what were Colonel Joe's losses?'

'None,' replied Mr Howlett. 'Only four wounded.'

The man got up to go. *'Erin go Bragh,'* he said with obvious satisfaction, and toasted the news of the victory by finishing his whiskey.

The others stood up now too. *'Erin go Bragh,'* they said, repeating the toast.

Erin go Bragh, Tom knew, was the watchword of the United Irishmen. It meant 'Ireland Forever' and adorned many of their flags.

With whispered words of good-bye, the men slipped out into the night and, speaking for the first time, Tom asked his parents, 'Do you really know Colonel Joe?'

Mr Howlett sucked on his pipe and nodded, 'Of course we do. Isn't he from this area?'

Mrs Howlett refilled her husband's glass, saying, 'But then you'd be too young to remember him.'

'What's he like?' asked Tom.

Mr Howlett smiled. 'Your mother seems to think he's handsome.'

'That's not what I said,' protested Mrs Howlett. 'I said some women might consider him to be good-looking.' She glanced over at Tom and smiled. 'Just the way I would consider your father to be good-looking.'

Tom knew that his father's work in the mill didn't allow him to pay much attention to his appearance, and the wide grin on his face showed that he was pleased with the compliment.

'He's about the same age too,' Mrs Howlett added. 'Forty or so.'

'He married a woman by the name of Hester Long up in Roundwood,' Mr Howlett continued. 'But the people here still regard him as one of their own.'

'Is it true that he once captured a notorious robber?' asked Tom.

Mr Howlett nodded. 'It is. His name was Rogers. Chased after him for miles, he did.'

'And how did he become a rebel?'

'The military burned his house up at Roundwood,' said Mrs Howlett. 'They said he tried to recruit two members of the Antrim Militia into the United Irishmen.'

'He escaped with only his sword and pistols,' continued Mr Howlett, 'and took refuge in the Devil's Glen. He recruited a lot more people there and now he's a force to be reckoned with.'

'What happened to his wife?' asked Tom.

'His wife and family are fine,' said Mrs Howlett. 'They move around from one hiding-place to another, but they're fine.'

'Is it true,' Tom asked, 'that Colonel Joe has vowed to get Hunter Gowan and the Black Mob?'

Mr Howlett lit up his pipe again and when he had pressed down the wriggling tobacco with his forefinger, he asserted, 'It's true all right. They're sworn enemies.'

'How come?'

'Because,' explained Mrs Howlett, 'Hunter Gowan has abused his position as a magistrate. He has done terrible things to people – just because he suspected them of supporting the United Irishmen.'

Mr Howlett laid down his pipe and taking a sip of whiskey recalled, 'In the week before the Rebellion began, he rode into Gorey at the head of his so-called yeomanry, with his sword drawn and a human finger stuck on the point of it?'

'Please,' said Mrs Howlett and, seeing that his wife was feeling a bit squeamish, Mr Howlett added, 'Anyway, Colonel Joe will put manners on him, just the way he put manners on the Ancient Britons at Ballyellis.'

Because of Colonel Holt's victory, Tom decided to keep a secret journal of events. However, if he or his family, or indeed their neighbours, were hoping that the tide was now turning in favour of the United Irishmen, they were soon to be disappointed.

From the bits and pieces of information given by passers-by, it emerged that after the battle of Ballyellis, the rebels had split up. Some of them had marched back into Wexford, but Colonel Holt had declined to join them, arguing that Wexford had been ravaged by the military and that provisions would be in short supply. He had then hoisted his colours and led over a thousand men back into the mountains of north Wicklow.

By this time, Tom knew, the rebel leader's reputation was higher than ever, and it rose even higher when his decision not to march into Wexford proved to be the right one.

2

Unexpected Visitors

○ We had just finished breakfast, Tom Howlett wrote in his journal, when we heard the sound of a horseman approaching the mill at great speed. My father knew immediately from the manner in which the horse was being ridden that something was wrong and ran out to the yard to meet him. I fastened my breeches and followed as fast as I could, arriving in the yard in time to see the horseman pull up with what seemed almost cruel abruptness. The horse was sweating profusely and frothing at the mouth, and the rider wasn't much better. His clothes were torn and bloodied, and he was in a considerable state of agitation.

As my father caught the horse by the reins to steady it up, the man told him in syllables of great breathlessness that the rebels who had crossed back into Wexford had been driven further south by two columns of the King's troops. Twice they had given battle, but the military had been too strong for them. Ammunition, it seemed, had also been in short supply. Forced to disperse, several thousand of them had retreated to the mountains and the long trek back up into Wicklow had begun. Hunger and hardship, he predicted, would be as big an enemy as the one they had just fought.

The man reined in his horse and, casting an anxious glance behind to make sure he wasn't being followed, said, 'They'll need all the help they can get.' Then, leaning forward, he lowered his voice and told my father, 'Try and get a message to Colonel Holt. He'll know what to do.' My father stepped back as the man spurred his horse forward saying, 'Got to go. The yeomen are on my heels.'

It was now my father's turn to cast an anxious glance

back up towards the road. 'Come on, Tom,' he said, and pushed me ahead of him towards the house. My mother, who had been watching from a discreet distance, motioned to us with an impatient gesture of her hand to hurry and, when she had ushered us inside, closed the door.

Our foreman, who had been getting his instructions for the day, was still in the house, and my father directed that he and Mary, our housekeeper, should join us in his study. By the time we had all joined him there, he had pushed his ledgers to one side of his desk and moved the family Bible over to the centre so that it was opposite his chair.

It has always been my father's custom to bring his family and workers together for a Bible reading on Sundays and on special occasions, such as harvest thanksgiving, but never before, as far as I can recall, did he have a reading early on the morning of a weekday.

Entitled *The Universal Family Bible,* ours is bound with brown leather and is a book of some considerable size and weight. From my perusal of the opening pages, I know that it contains the Old and New Testaments, and that it was printed by someone called Zacharia Jackson in Dublin in 1793. Yet these matters were far from my mind as I watched my father open it, and it was no surprise when he turned to the last book in the New Testament, The Revelation of St John the Divine.

It was to Revelations that my father had often turned before, especially when bad weather was likely to produce a bad harvest. Perhaps its dreadful vision of how the world would end suited his mood. Little did I know that he had a particular reason for turning to the Book of Revelations now, and that my very life would depend on my familiarity with its contents.

'...And round about the throne,' my father read, 'were four beasts full of eyes before and behind. And the first beast was like a lion, and the second beast like a calf, and the third beast had the face as a man, and the fourth beast was like a flying eagle...'

My father paused for a moment, and I could see he was turning an ear to the road. Hearing nothing, he continued, 'And I saw on the right hand of him that sat on the throne a book written within and on the back side, sealed with seven seals... And lo in the midst of the throne and of the four beasts, and in the midst of the elders, stood a lamb as it had been slain, having seven horns and seven eyes, which are the seven spirits of God sent forth into all the earth.'

The sound of flailing hooves now made all of us look up towards the road, and I suspected that my father was skipping bits when he went on to read, 'And I saw when the lamb opened one of the seals, and I heard as it were the noise of thunder, one of the four beasts saying, "Come and see."'

From the pounding of the hooves it was clear that several horsemen had come thundering into the yard, but my father continued, and when he did so I knew for certain that he was being selective in what he was reading,

'And when he had opened the third seal, I heard the third beast say, "Come and see." And I beheld, and lo a black horse; and he that sat on him had a pair of balances in his hand...'

It was at this stage that I always imagined Hunter Gowan and the Black Mob riding down upon us to exact revenge for our support of the United Irishmen. Furthermore, I was now haunted by my father's account of how the renegade magistrate had made a triumphal entry into Gorey with the finger stuck on the point of his sword. That was something which, by all accounts, had even disgusted the military. My father had assured me it was nothing compared to the pillage and slaughter that followed as Hunter Gowan and his gang acted as judge, jury and executioner. However, the image of the finger on the sword was something I could not get out of my mind.

The Bible reading interrupted

There was a loud banging on the door now, and when my mother answered it she returned with several members of the yeomen cavalry. Somehow their brightly buttoned blue tunics, heavy riding-boots and jangling sabres seemed oddly out of place at a Bible reading.

Seeing that my father had stopped reading and was looking up to see what they wanted, the young lieutenant in charge removed his furry helmet and, tucking it under his left arm, observed, 'A strange time to be consulting the Good Book.'

'Its message is good,' my father replied, 'no matter when you consult it.'

The officer, I could see, wasn't quite sure of his ground. He had obviously guessed that my father, being a miller and, in all probability, a landowner, was most likely a member of the established Church, in other words a Protestant. The reading of the family Bible would have reinforced this view. At the same time, he would be well aware that the loyalty of no one could be taken for granted, as the United Irishmen had sought to unite Catholic, Protestant and Dissenter. Some prominent members of the established Church had even become their leaders.

My father, I sensed, wasn't sure of his ground either. The yeoman were, in effect, private armies of the very wealthy, the people with big estates. They had proved to be ruthless, often dispensing with trials and hanging people who, for one reason or another, they hadn't put to the sword. The lettering on their helmets indicated that they were from another area, so he could expect to be treated as a stranger.

'Anyway,' my father added, closing the Bible, 'we find it lays a good foundation for the day.'

The officer nodded. 'Have you seen a rider pass this way?'

My father nodded. 'We did indeed. Why, who was he?'

'A rebel.' The officer turned to go, saying, 'Mind if we

have a look around?'

Knowing that they would have a look around whether he minded or not, my father replied, 'Not at all,' and followed them out into the yard. As they walked up towards the mill, my mother told me to get ready for school, and directed the foreman and the maid to go about their day's work. We all knew there were several wounded rebels hidden in the dark recesses of the mill, but we reckoned the yeomen wouldn't want to dirty their brightly coloured tunics or white breeches by looking too hard. Nevertheless, we breathed a sigh of relief when, a short time later, we saw them mounting up and galloping off in pursuit of our early morning caller.

It was then my father told us that someone would have to get a message to Colonel Holt. The question was who? O

3

A Dangerous Mission

'One thing for certain,' Mrs Howlett told her husband, 'you can't go. You've a mill to run.'

Mr Howlett nodded. 'I know. Unless I get one of the men to go?'

'We've few enough as it is,' Mrs Howlett reminded him.

'They'd have to get past Hunter Gowan and his gang,' said Tom.

Mr Howlett shook his head. 'Hunter Gowan is more likely to be doing his dirty work down in Wexford.'

'Maybe then,' Tom suggested, 'I could do it.'

'Don't be silly,' said his mother. 'Of course you couldn't. You're only a boy. Anyway, it would be too dangerous.'

'Not if I took Betsy,' Tom protested. 'I'd be in north Wicklow by evening.'

Mr Howlett looked hard at his son, saying, 'Tom, do you really think you could do it?'

Mrs Howlett turned to her husband. 'You can't be serious. He's only a boy.'

Mr Howlett nodded. 'I am serious. This is a serious situation and it just might be that a boy would get through where a man wouldn't. He wouldn't arouse the same suspicion.'

Mrs Howlett still didn't like the idea and it was only because so many lives depended on it that she eventually agreed. As she hurried into the house to get Tom some food for the journey, his father brought out the mare.

'I know she's only a cart-horse,' said Mr Howlett, 'and she's pretty old, but she'll get you there if you treat her right.' He adjusted the halter and lifted the reins over her head. 'Now, here's what you have to do. Follow the

Avonbeg River until you come to Glenmalure. With luck you'll find Michael Dwyer and his men there. You've met Captain Dwyer before, so he'll know who you are. Tell him to prepare for the wounded. And then head straight on towards Blessington. You'll find Colonel Joe's camp at Whelp Rock overlooking Blessington. Tell him to prepare to receive the others.'

Tom nodded.

'And here's your school-bag,' said his mother. 'I've put enough food into it to keep you going until you get there.'

'Good idea,' said his father. 'It'll also give you an excuse if anyone stops you.'

'How do you mean?' asked Tom.

'I mean, you can make up a story about being on your way to school, or to visit relatives, depending on where you are at the time. You'll just have to make something up.'

'And how will I know Colonel Joe?'

'That shouldn't be a problem,' his father assured him. 'The letters JH are on his flag. And I've given you the password. He'll have the rest of it. Anyway, once you tell him who you are, you should be all right.'

As Betsy was a cart-horse, they didn't have a saddle for her. However, Tom was used to riding her bareback and after his mother had given him a hug and told him to be very very careful, his father gave him a leg up.

'Don't forget,' his father called after him. 'A lot of lives depend on you.'

Holding on to his hat with one hand, and the reins with the other, Tom urged Betsy into a gallop and headed up along the Avoca River to where it was joined by the Avonbeg.

To those involved in the rebellion, Glenmalure was, for a time at least, a place of refuge. The man who defended it, Michael Dwyer, did so with great determination and was often referred to as the Governor of Glenmalure. Many weak, sickly and wounded were known to be under his care. It was also a place where stragglers and those suffering from fatigue could rest and recover.

For this reason and to forewarn of any danger, rebel scouts were always on the look-out, with the result that they found Tom Howlett before he could find them. Recognising two of them as being from the village of Newbridge, he gave them the message which they undertook to convey immediately to Michael Dwyer.

As the scouts led the way up to the head of the glen, they spoke in excited terms about the victory at Ballyellis. It was, Tom felt, almost as if they were trying to compensate in their own minds for the bad news that they had now heard. For the first time, he learned that Michael Dwyer had taken part in the ambush at Ballyellis, although the scouts were fulsome in their praise of Colonel Holt who, they acknowledged, had planned it. Before parting, they thanked him, wished him well and advised him on the best route to take to get to Whelp Rock.

As Tom continued his journey, he had no way of knowing that those who served Colonel Holt would not be so friendly as those who served the Governor of Glenmalure. Nor would some of the people he would encounter along the way.

It was a lovely sunny day but the signs of rebellion were everywhere, even, it seemed, in the remotest upland hills. Here and there, unexpected hollows opened up to reveal families crouching around the few worldly goods they had been able to salvage from whatever disaster had befallen them. There was, he could see, fear in their eyes and hunger in their fragile bodies. And once, when several half-crazed creatures came from nowhere to claw at Betsy's bridle and the satchel that hung from his shoulder, he escaped from their clutches only because he had the presence of mind to throw them pieces of food.

Tom was sorry to see people in such a plight, but he was afraid of them too, so he urged Betsy on and didn't stop until he found himself in the relative safety of the mountains. There he stopped beside a small cluster of lakes and, when he dismounted, he led the mare to the edge of the water where they both slaked their thirst.

The sun was high now and it was very warm. Afraid that if Betsy drank too much her belly might get even more swollen than it was, Tom pulled her away from the lake and led her along the shore to give her a rest. Now and then the sound of distant musket-shots broke the silence, but he knew that sounds carried far in the mountains and, seeing no sign of a red tunic anywhere in the surrounding hills, he kept going.

At the same time, Tom couldn't help wondering if a detachment of the King's troops might be over the next rise. It was a thought that gave him considerable unease, for as the Rebellion had spread, so too had the activities of the military. House burnings, torture, floggings and executions had become commonplace as the authorities tried to find out what was going on and to frighten those who might be tempted to support the rebels. One thing had borrowed another and it wasn't long before those suspected of loyalty to the United Irishmen on the one hand, and those suspected of loyalty to the Crown on the other, were receiving the same treatment. Life had become cheap, trials rare, punishment swift.

So preoccupied was Tom with thoughts of what might lie ahead of him that he was completely taken by surprise by the sound of horses' hooves coming up behind him. Looking back, he saw a number of men galloping towards him. It was clear at a glance that they were not members of the military, for instead of brightly coloured tunics, they wore ordinary clothes. Their coats were flapping as they spurred their horses on and the leading horseman was pointing the way forward with a pistol.

Thinking that they might be members of Colonel Joe's forces, Tom looked beyond them to see who might be chasing them, but saw no one. Why then, were they

riding so fast? he wondered. Unless they were chasing
someone. But who? There was no one else around as far
as he could see. As the riders drew nearer, he saw that
their leader was a heavy-set man. He wore a short black
coat and a round black hat.

Suddenly the realisation came crashing in on Tom's
mind that he was looking at none other than the in-
famous Hunter Gowan and his gang, the notorious Black
Mob. Furthermore, they were bearing down on him with
unrelenting speed and a purpose that was now all too
obvious. They were chasing *him*! Grasping Betsy's mane
with both hands, he pulled himself up on to her back
and, with a cry of 'C'mon Betsy, let's get out of here,' he
dug his heels into her sides. Surprised by the unusual
vigour with which her young rider had treated her, the
mare sprang into action and took off along the lake
shore.

Tom was aware that his arms and legs were flailing all
over the place as he urged the mare on. Yet, despite his
urgings, he knew in his heart and soul that she would
never be able to outrun his pursuers. What would happen
when they caught up with him? he wondered. Would they
kill him, or take him prisoner? Would they torture him to
make him disclose the purpose of his mission? And what
would happen if he told them? The survivors of the
Wexford expedition would be intercepted and killed.
Even if he didn't tell, they would die of hunger. Either
way, he reckoned, it would be torture for him. When he
thought of that, he had visions of Hunter Gowan making
a triumphal entry into Newbridge, displaying on the point
of his sword the finger of the young rebel messenger he
had just hunted down. It was a thought that made him
feel like getting sick, and he urged Betsy on to even
greater speed.

Betsy was beginning to slow down when a shot rang
out. Thinking it was a warning shot to make him stop,
Tom looked back. He was expecting to find the Black

Mob almost on top of him. Instead, to his surprise, he saw them wheeling around and galloping back the way they had come. At the same time he saw another, larger group of horsemen come sliding down the side of the valley. Without as much as a glance at him they rode off in pursuit of the Black Mob, firing their pistols as they went.

Wondering what was going on, Tom brought Betsy to a halt and slid to the ground. He was trembling so much he could hardly stand. Poor Betsy, he could see, wasn't much better, so he calmed her down as best he could and waited anxiously to see what the outcome of the running battle was going to be.

As the horsemen faded into the distance, the shooting continued. Then a group of them returned, and Tom breathed a sign of relief when he saw that the Black Mob had been put to flight. However, his relief was short-lived. While the new arrivals wore various types of jackets, and bristled with pistols and swords, the horses and their harness obviously belonged to the military.

The leader of the group was a tall young man with flaming red hair and a freckled face. He spoke with a distinctly north of Ireland accent and Tom couldn't help wondering if, perhaps, he was associated with the Antrim Militia who were stationed in various parts of the county. 'Who are you, and what are you doing here?' he demanded.

Not knowing where the nearest town might be, Tom decided it would be useless pretending he was going to visit relatives, so he replied, 'My name's Tom Howlett. I'm from Newbridge ... near the Avoca River.'

'And what's in that satchel you have?' asked another of the group.

'It's my school-bag,' Tom told him and, taking if off, handed it over. 'I brought something to eat in it.'

As the others rifled the contents of the bag, the man with the red hair asked, 'What are you doing up here?

You're a long way from home.'

It now occurred to Tom that these might be some of Colonel Holt's men and that they had acquired the horses when they had ambushed the cavalrymen at Ballyellis. So he decided to use the password his father had given him. 'I'm looking for a black horse,' he replied. When there was no reaction, he added, 'It's always wandering off on us. My father asked me to look for it.'

One of the group drew his pistol and, cocking it, asked him, 'You wouldn't be looking for rebels by any chance? Maybe spying for the military?'

'I told you,' Tom protested. 'I'm looking for a black horse.' Again there was no reaction to the password, and in desperation he asked, 'Why would the Black Mob be chasing me if I was spying for the Crown?'

'So why *were* they chasing you then?' asked another.

Tom shook his head. 'I just don't know. Why were *you* chasing them?'

'There you are,' shouted one of the riders farther back. 'He *is* a spy. He's trying to find out who we are?'

On hearing that, several of the group drew their pistols and Tom was quite certain they would have shot him on the spot had the man with the red hair not intervened. 'Enough of that,' he told them. 'If he's a spy he'll get a fair trial – then we'll shoot him.' Turning to Tom, he ordered him to mount up and, taking the reins, led Betsy alongside his own horse as they headed up into the hills.

For his part, Tom could only hold on to Betsy's mane – and the hope that if his captors were Colonel Holt's men someone somewhere would recognise the password his father had given him.

4

Behold a Black Horse

It was coming on to evening when Tom's captors stopped in a small glen in the foothills of the mountains and dismounted. The red-haired man told Tom to do likewise and sat him down under a rowanberry-tree which grew nearby. He then instructed the others to tend to their horses and mounted up again. 'I'll go on ahead and find out what has to be done with the boy,' he told them. As he turned to go, he added, 'And make sure no harm comes to him until I come back. I won't be long.'

It was only when Tom shifted his position under the rowanberry-tree, that he realised how sore his backside was from all the bouncing about on Betsy's bony back. However, that was the least of his worries. He reckoned that his captors had stopped short of their camp so that he wouldn't know where it was located, and he couldn't help wondering what they were going do with him. He was comforted by the fact that the group's leader had left instructions that he wasn't to be harmed, but it was a comfort that was short-lived. It wasn't long before he found that there was little or no discipline in the group, and the instruction they had been given counted for very little.

When there was no sign of their friend returning, the other members of the group began to get restless. At first it appeared that they were merely curious.

'Is your name really Howlett?' one wanted to know. The questioner was a scraggy little man with a grin that revealed a mouthful of bad teeth.

Tom assured him it was, but the man wanted to know more. Where exactly did his people live? Was he a Protestant by any chance?

Knowing that the majority of the rebels were Catholics

31

Rescued by Antrim John

CITY OF LIMERICK PUBLIC LIBRARY

and that many members of the Protestant population were Orangemen who were loyal to the Crown, Tom replied no, that he was a Catholic.

The man was now toying with his pistol, which Tom could see was at half-cock. Concerned at the way things were going, he pretended to bless himself, hoping against hope that they wouldn't harm him before the red-haired man came back.

Hearing what had been said another man stepped forward, drew his pistol and, putting the muzzle to the side of Tom's head, said, 'Since when did they allow Catholic boys to go to school?'

'And on their own horse?' grinned the man with the bad teeth.

Sensing that all was not right with the replies that were being given, the others were crowding around now too. Next thing Tom knew, one of them fired a pistol at him. As he ducked he heard the ball whizzing over his head and embedding itself in the trunk of the rowanberry-tree. At the same time they rushed towards him and were pulling him to his feet when there was another pistol-shot.

Looking up, Tom saw, to his great relief, that the red-haired man had returned. He now berated the others for disobeying his instructions and would have trampled them with his horse had they not moved aside.

'I told you the boy wasn't to be harmed,' he shouted and, turning his horse around so that he was facing them, added, 'Now back off. The Colonel wants to see him.'

Having tucked his pistol into his belt, the red-haired man pulled Tom up behind him and spurred his horse up the side of the glen. As they approached a hill not far away, two armed men who were sitting on an outcrop of rock, apparently on look-out duty, waved them on. Tom hung on tightly as the man, using various twisting paths, urged his horse to the top of the hill. There he stopped to allow the horse to rest and Tom could see that a wide, wooded valley lay before them. Picking his way with care,

B 42707

the man eased his horse down the slope and it was only then, as they entered the trees, that Tom realised the valley was one huge rebel camp. Beneath the trees and bushes, groups of men, women and children were gathered around cooking-pots and numerous makeshift tents. Green flags flew from many of the tent poles and here and there, beside their belongings, were stacks of muskets and long-handled pikes.

The red-haired man didn't stop until he arrived at a cluster of tents, before which stood a number of men. Most of them, Tom observed, were wearing uniforms of one kind or another. Some of the uniforms were green, others grey, and several of them appeared to him to have been somewhat crudely made. As he was ushered over to the men, he became aware once again that his backside was sore. He was also tired and hungry and in a state of considerable anxiety as he was fearful of what his fate was going to be.

One man in the centre of the group seemed to stand out. Unlike the others, he didn't wear a uniform, just an open-necked shirt and breeches, but he was of strong build and commanding appearance. In the belt of his breeches were tucked two silver-mounted pistols and at his side hung a silver-mounted sword. Standing with his hands on his hips, legs firmly apart, he fixed Tom with his dark, penetrating eyes, and asked, 'What's your name, boy?'

'Tom Howlett of Newbridge.'

The man's eyes narrowed, as if the name had struck a chord, and Tom wondered if this was Colonel Holt. He had short black receding hair, some of which curled forward on to a high brow, and he wore his beard under his chin. This all tended to highlight his face and Tom was trying to decide if it was a face that his mother would call handsome when the man asked, 'And your father?'

'He's Tom too. He's a miller.'

'And what are you doing up here?'

'I'm looking for a black horse,' Tom told him.

'So I hear,' the man said. 'Come with me.'

The others stood aside and waited as the man took Tom into his tent and offered him a chair. Tom thanked him but declined, explaining that he was sore from having ridden so far, bareback. The man then seated himself at a small table on which lay a large Bible. He was watching Tom carefully, and seeing him glance at the Bible asked, 'Are you familiar with God's word?'

Almost certain now that he was in the presence of Colonel Holt, Tom nodded, saying, 'Some of it.'

Opening the Bible, the man proceeded to read: 'And when he had opened the third seal, I heard the third beast say, "Come and see..."'

When he stopped and looked up, Tom said, 'And I beheld, and lo a black horse.'

The man smiled, and continued the quotation: 'And he that sat on him had a pair of balances in his hand.'

Tom was smiling now too. 'And I heard a voice in the midst of the four beasts say...'

The man closed the Bible, adding, 'A measure of wheat for a penny...'

Tom joined in so that they completed the quotation with one voice, 'And three measures of barley for a penny.'

Reaching out his hand, the man took Tom's and shook it warmly, saying, 'Welcome to Whelp Rock.'

'Colonel Holt?' Tom felt like throwing his arms around him, he was so pleased. 'Is it really you?'

'Of course. Who else would know the password from the Book of Revelations?' The rebel leader smiled. 'Now, tell me your story.'

As soon as Colonel Holt heard that the Wexford forces had been dispersed and that several thousand survivors were now on their way to join him, he excused himself and went outside. There he relayed the information to his officers and instructed them to range far and wide for supplies of food. When he returned, he told Tom not to be afraid, saying, 'No one will harm you. You will be under my protection.' He then ordered some food for him and, while they were waiting for it to come, asked him about his encounter with Hunter Gowan and the Black Mob.

'They must have suspected that I was a messenger,' Tom told him.

The rebel leader nodded. 'A lone rider in the hills, a satchel on your shoulder. They probably thought you were carrying papers of some sort.'

'I was lucky your men came along,' said Tom. 'Otherwise I was finished.'

'Some day,' Colonel Joe told him, 'some day I'll put manners on my brave Hunter Gowan. He has said he'll make a sixpenny loaf be sufficient for me and my men. But we'll see. We'll see. In the meantime, Tom, I don't think it would be safe for you to try to return home – at least, not for a week or so.'

Tom agreed. He didn't fancy the idea of having to run the gauntlet with Hunter Gowan and his gang a second time.

Colonel Holt then told him that it was his custom to place what he called 'every new recruit' under the care of a trusted person.

Tom immediately requested that he be placed under the care of the red-haired man who had saved his life.

Colonel Holt smiled, saying, 'Ah, Antrim John. He's one of my most trusted lieutenants. Very well, from now on, if you're not with me, you'll be with him.' He was now leafing through Tom's school-books which had been delivered to the tent, and observed, 'You can read and write, I see.'

'Of course,' said Tom, 'I go to the parish school in Newbridge.'

'Is your father still running the mill?'

Tom nodded. 'He told me he knew you.'

Colonel Holt got to his feet. 'Tom,' he said, 'I can see you're a smart lad, and one that can be trusted. How would you like to be my *aide-de-camp?*'

Tom was taken aback. 'What would I have to do?' he asked.

Rummaging among a pile of personal effects in the corner of the tent, Colonel Holt produced a quill and a jar of ink. 'I never was much good at this writing business,' he confessed. 'Maybe you could handle it for me. You know, messages, letters, that kind of thing.'

'And can I keep a journal?' Tom asked him.

'Well,' he said, 'I suppose you can – but don't write too many secrets in it!'

O When I inquired, Tom wrote in his journal, I was informed that Antrim John had got his name from the fact that he had been in the Antrim Militia. Later, when more members of the same regiment deserted, there would be several Antrim Johns. However, as far as I was concerned there was only one – the tall red-haired protector who had twice saved my life.

As we got to know each other, Antrim John told me I was right in assuming that they had got their horses from the cavalrymen they has ambushed at Ballyellis. Normally, he said, only their leaders and a few others were mounted, as horses were needed to draw the carts with provisions and wounded. However, the defeat of the Ancient Britons had provided them not only with a much-needed victory but a big number of horses, as well as the cavalrymen's short muskets called carbines, swords, pistols and a welcome supply of ball cartridges.

Acting on my information, Colonel Joe sent out a party of his men on his best horses to forage for food. They went in all directions and it wasn't long before they began to return with both food and the utensils in which to cook it. First they arrived with two metal boilers. Seventy-nine head of cattle followed, then six calves, six large swine, sacks of oatmeal and potatoes. Colonel Joe even ordered his men to search all houses within a four-mile radius for salt, and then he set his butchers to work.

While all this was being done, others had been busy collecting firewood. As it had been a very hot summer, there was plenty of dry wood to be found and in no time at all the beef had been boiled, cut up into small pieces and put into dishes. The result was that when the columns of men from Wexford arrived at Whelp Rock, there was plenty of food for all of them.

Apart from hunger, the newcomers were suffering from fatigue and Colonel Joe ordered that they should rest. Then, when they had recovered, he organised a series of training exercises. These exercises, or manoeuvres, as he called them, were conducted by Antrim John and others with military experience. They involved sham battles in which pikes, muskets and other weapons were used. Apart from the training involved, these battles relieved the boredom which many of Colonel Joe's men had come to feel. They were also great fun and were entered into with enthusiasm by all concerned, including the many young people who were among the camp-followers.

Soon, word spread that the leaders whose forces were gathered at Whelp Rock had called a meeting. It was then that the fun came to an end. O

5

A Council of War

Looking down the valley, Tom could see a much deeper valley beyond it and, beyond that, the little village of Blessington. He was standing on a rock with Antrim John, who was pointing out various features of the surrounding countryside. The grey, stony hill on the left, he learned, was Whelp Rock.

'But why do you have a camp here, so near Dublin?' Tom asked, when he learned that the city was only about eighteen miles away.

'Because,' said Antrim John, 'this is Colonel Holt's area. This, and the whole of north Wicklow. And when the day comes that we have to attack the capital, he'll be the one who'll do it.'

As they moved about the camp, Tom found that it was absolutely crammed with rebels and their families. Some of the womenfolk were busy making, or mending, flags of various colours and descriptions. Seeing a group of men attaching a flag, about two foot high, to a new standard, he stopped to watch. A few minutes later they unrolled it across the grass and he saw that it wasn't square, but in the shape of a triangle about eight foot long.

'That's what we call a pennant,' said Antrim John.

Tom could now see that the overall colour of the pennant was green and that it was fringed with gold. It was decorated with a gold harp, above which were the words, God Save Ireland. These emblems were wreathed in gold shamrocks, as was the large gold lettering that stretched all the way to the tip.

'Whitechurch,' said Tom to himself, as he read the lettering

'They're from Wexford,' Antrim John told him.

Moving on, Tom said, 'I've never seen so many people

in the one place. How many do you think there are?'

Antrim John stopped again and, looking around the camp, said, 'Five, six, seven thousand – who knows?'

'There's an awful lot, all right.'

'Aye, an awful lot. But the question is, how many of them will keep on fighting?'

'Is it not dangerous to have women and children here in the camp?'

'Maybe, but I suppose they feel safer with us. You see, if they're at home and the menfolk are not, the military will know they're rebels and burn their cabins.'

So vast indeed were the numbers gathered at Whelp Rock that Antrim John warned Tom not to be moving about on his own. 'There are a number of armies here now,' he said. 'They're from different areas, and if you go wandering around asking questions they'll think you're a spy. You won't have a chance. They'll just kill you and there'd be nothing either I or Colonel Holt could do.'

'Why do you think they've called this meeting?' asked Tom.

'It's more than a meeting,' Antrim John told him. 'It's a Council of War.'

'Do you think it's to plan an attack on Dublin?'

Antrim John shook his head. 'I don't know. But, being the Colonel's *aide-de-camp*, I reckon you'll know before I do.'

○ The council of war, Tom recorded in his journal, was held that night when officers of the various armies gathered around a camp-fire in a secluded area not far from General Joe's tent. Armed men were posted at various locations to ensure that no one intruded upon their deliberations, or overheard what was being said.

With the arrival of the rebels from Wexford, there were a large number of officers at Whelp Rock, and no fewer than twenty-four of them now consulted with Colonel Joe as to what was the best course of action to take. The leaders, so far as I can recall, were Garret Byrne, Edward Fitzgerald, Anthony Perry, Esmond Kyan and Father Mogue Kearns. Their followers spoke of them with great admiration, as they had been through a lot of battles together. What their ranks were, I cannot recall, but I was told that the first two were young Catholic gentlemen, Mr Byrne being from Ballymanus in County Wicklow and Mr Fitzgerald from Newpark in County Wexford. The other three I remember for vastly different reasons.

Mr Perry used to live across the border in County Wexford, not far from where we lived in the Avoca valley, and his head was grossly scarred as a result of having been treated in the most barbarous manner. Even though he was a Protestant from the north of Ireland and a gentleman of amiable manners, he had been arrested on suspicion of conspiring with the United Irishmen and pitch-capped. This, I was told, involved putting a cap made of pitch and gunpowder on his head and setting it alight. Pitch-capping had been invented by a sergeant of the North Cork Militia called Tom the Devil, although whether he himself carried out the torture on Mr Perry, I cannot say.

Poor Esmond Kyan, I recall, simply because he was wounded. A small man, he had, I was told, lost much of his left arm in an accident and wore a cork one in its place. Then, as fate would have it, a cannon-ball had carried away even more of his arm during the battle of Arklow the previous month. How he managed to continue with the rebel army, I do not know, as he was not a well man.

Unlike Mr Kyan, Father Kearns was a man of extraordinary size. In conversations with Antrim John and myself, many of those who had accompanied the priest from Wexford had spoken of his great strength and ferocity. Not surprisingly, the stories about him were legion, but the one that fascinated me most related to a time when he was in France. The Roman clergy, I gather,

were not very popular with the French and they tried to
hang him from a lamp-post in Paris. However, his great
weight was said to have bent the post to the extent that
his toes had touched the ground. Seeing his plight, an
Irish doctor had cut him down and taken him to his
house to recover. Father Kearns had then fled to Ireland
where he had become a curate near Clonard in County
Meath.

We didn't know it then, but it was this connection with
Clonard that was to be our undoing.

When the council of war got under way, Colonel Joe
proposed that they should march eastwards over the
mountains to Newtownmountkennedy where the garrison
had ammunition and two of what he called field pieces.
After seizing these, he said, they could march to Wicklow,
free prisoners being held there, and then proceed to Dublin.

However, Father Kearns opposed this plan, proposing
instead that they should march northwards and attack the
house of the High Sheriff of Kildare. The house, he said,
was at Clonard, on the Kildare-Meath border. Their
numbers, he believed, would be greatly augmented by
recruits who would join them along the way, and there
was a large quantity of guns and ammunition to be seized
from the Sheriff's armoury.

From the initial silence with which the priest's proposal
was received, I sensed that the other leaders present at the
council of war realised that they would be taking a great
gamble, for once they left the mountains they would be in
the open countryside. Nevertheless, the two proposals
were discussed at length. A good many leaders backed
Colonel Joe and expressed reservations about the wisdom
of attacking the Sheriff's House. Others argued equally
strongly in favour of the priest's plan, saying that after the
attack, they could press on and rouse counties that had
not taken part in the Rebellion. There were also voices,
on both sides, that spoke of holding out until the French
arrived to support them. As I listened to the arguments

that were made for and against the proposals, I could not imagine which of them would be adopted. Eventually, however, they were put to a vote, and the proposal made by Father Kearns was carried by the narrow margin of two.

The leaders now began to discuss the finer details of the priest's plan. Before attacking Clonard, the suggestion was that they would link up with the rebel forces in Kildare which, I gathered, were commanded by yet another leader, a man called William Aylmer. The hour was late now and I was tired, so I returned to my tent. As I went to bed, I couldn't help wondering what the next few days would bring. Had I known, I would have stolen away that night and returned to my home in the Avoca valley. Fortunately, I had no way of knowing the fate that was to befall us, and I slept until the noise of great activity in the camp awakened me next morning. ○

News of what had been decided spread quickly through the rebel forces and at dawn the next day preparations for the expedition got under way. Everyone was busy and horsemen were coming and going at a gallop as messages were relayed from one army to another.

Each of the leaders saw to his own men and, as Colonel Holt walked among his, Tom asked him what he had meant by his proposal that they should seize ammunition and two field pieces from the garrison at Newtownmount-kennedy?

'I mean, what are field pieces?' he asked.

'They're pieces of artillery,' Colonel Holt told him. 'Like cannon. They're mounted on two wheels and in a battle can be used with great effect. Time and again small numbers of Crown forces retreat to the safety of stone buildings and we can't dislodge them. With those two field pieces it would be different. Cannon-balls will tear a building apart and, if they're loaded with grapeshot, they can devastate a whole army of soldiers.'

'What's grapeshot?' asked Tom

'Small balls or bits and pieces of iron. They'll mow down the enemy like stalks of corn.'

Tom shivered. 'Sounds terrible.'

'War *is* terrible,' replied Colonel Holt.

'And where exactly will we go if the attack on the Sheriff's House at Clonard is successful?'

Colonel Holt stopped and, looking around to make sure he couldn't be overheard, said, 'Between you and me, Tom, what worries me is, where will we go if it's not.'

Tom now found that there was an air of tension among the rebels. Gone was their restful, easy-going manner of the past few days. The sham battles were a thing of the past. Ahead of them, they knew, lay the real thing. As a result, they were more suspicious of strangers than ever, and Tom wasn't surprised to hear that someone had been detained, accused of being a spy. His own experience, when he had almost been shot because of the same suspicion, was still fresh in his mind, and he was glad that Colonel Holt was by his side.

At the same time, others who were strangers to Tom seemed to be able to come and go as they pleased. One was a very good-looking young woman who moved freely through the camp with a distinctly devil-may-care attitude. As she passed from one group of rebels to another, many of them greeted here with a wave and a smile. Where there were women-folk, however, they gave her a less friendly reception and made her move on.

'Dolan's her name,' said Colonel Holt before Tom could ask. 'She's a camp-follower from Carnew.'

Looking up, Tom saw that he was smiling, as if the sight of such a pretty young woman didn't displease him.

'Her friends call her Bridget,' he added.

'And the others?'

Colonel Holt was still smiling. 'I hear that those who don't approve of her – or of the Rebellion – call her Croppy Biddy.'

Colonel Joe introduces Tom to Croppy Biddy

Tom was puzzled. 'How come?'

'Well, as you know, many of us crop our hair, the same way as the French did during their rebellion. That's why our enemies call us Croppies. And because she's a camp-follower, people who don't approve of her fraternising with us call her Croppy Biddy.'

As Colonel Holt turned to go, it seemed to Tom that the young woman was returning his smile. By now, however, he had other things on his mind. Many of the rebels were crouching around fires, melting lead for making ball cartridges, and he stopped here and there to give them words of encouragement. When the balls had cooled, they were duly distributed to those in need of ammunition. It was a fascinating process and Tom was watching it when, to his surprise, a woman wearing a long dark cloak joined them. She was stooped and her face was hidden by her hood, but she aroused not the slightest suspicion among the rebels. Instead, she straightened up and engaged Colonel Holt in a whispered conversation, after which she walked with him back to his tent.

Tom followed and, if he was surprised at the appearance of the hooded figure, he was even more surprised when, from beneath her voluminous petticoats, she extracted two large bags. Leaving them at the feet of Antrim John, she bent down and walked into the tent with Colonel Holt. Antrim John lifted one bag in each hand and, seeing how heavy they seemed to be, Tom asked, 'What's in them?'

'Ball cartridges,' Antrim John told him. 'And maybe some gunpowder.'

As the cartridges were distributed, Tom counted no fewer than three hundred. 'But how does she manage to carry so many?' he asked. 'They're made of solid lead?'

Antrim John smiled. 'Well, you wouldn't think it, but she's a very strong woman.' Looking towards the tent, he lowered his voice in case she might reappear. 'They say she's the daughter of a blacksmith and that she handles the sledge-hammer as well as any man.'

'But why does she cover her face with a hood?'

Antrim John cast another glance towards the tent. 'To hide her broken nose. They say it was smashed by a stone during a faction fight.'

'And where does she get the cartridges?'

'From disaffected members of the militia. She's only about thirty but when she stoops and puts on a face, you'd think she was an old woman. She also sells fruit and gingerbread from her baskets. That way she can wander through the enemy camps without arousing suspicion.'

'And what's she doing talking to Colonel Joe?'

Antrim John leaned a little closer. 'Well, it's not only cartridges she collects. She gathers a lot of information too. Important information about the movements of the Crown troops. That's worth even more to Colonel Holt than cartridges.'

'What's her name?' asked Tom.

Antrim John shook his head. 'Who knows? Colonel Joe just calls her his Moving Magazine – you know, on account of all the ammunition she stores under her cloak.'

Tom couldn't help wondering how a woman who covered her head and face with a hood could walk through the enemy camps without arousing suspicion. Either she was very good at being a spy, he thought, or she was very lucky.

Less lucky, Tom discovered, was the person who was detained by the rebels a short time earlier and brought before Colonel Holt on suspicion that he was spying on their camp.

6

A Pair of Balances

○ To my dismay, Tom wrote in his journal, I found that the person accused of being a spy was only a boy, about the same age as myself. When Colonel Joe asked him what he was doing, he replied that he was looking for his father, James Connor from Hacketstown. However, inquiries established that there was no such person in the camp. Then, someone recognised him as the son of a basket-woman called Murphy. Realising that he had been telling lies, Colonel Joe ordered him to be whipped. After receiving three lashes he confessed that he had been sent by a Captain McDonnell to observe the situation in the camp. The captain had given him three guineas, which he had given to his mother, and a promise of a suit of clothes if he supplied the information.

Without further delay, the boy was taken away and tried for spying. I was not present at the trial and, when Colonel Joe returned, I asked him what the outcome had been. Sitting down at the table in his tent, he leaned forward as if there was a great weight on his shoulders and, without looking up, told me, 'He's been found guilty.'

'What will happen to him?' I asked.

'There's only one sentence for spying – he's been sentenced to death.'

'But you can't execute him,' I protested. 'He's only eleven.'

'Tom,' said Colonel Joe. 'I have a son the same age. His name is Joshua. So you can imagine how I feel.' He sighed. 'But that's not the point. You see, if we punish the boy and release him, he'll go straight to the military and tell them what he has seen. That will mean death for many of us. Maybe even death for you if he points you out some day. In any case, my men wouldn't allow me to release him.'

'But you're their leader,' I argued.

'I am,' Colonel Joe replied, 'but only so long as they'll follow me. You see, they're not a disciplined army, not in the same way that the forces of the Crown are. They're cottagers, peasants, at best small farmers, and above all, Catholics. When things go right, as at Ballyellis, they see me as a great leader. When things go wrong they remember that I'm a Protestant and distrust me. There have even been occasions when the word has been spread that my wife's family are Orangemen.'

Colonel Joe had his right hand on the Bible now, and I couldn't help thinking that he was like the man on the black horse, the man with a pair of balances in his hand, the scales of justice.

'If I reprieved the boy,' he added, 'I would be condemning my own men to death, maybe even their families too, and I can't do that.'

How and when the execution was carried out, I do not know, but I often wonder if Captain McDonnell ever became aware of the high price his young spy had to pay in return for the princely sum of three guineas and a promise of a suit of clothes. ○

7

The Sheriff's House

George Tyrell pulled up a chair in the drawing-room of his father's mansion at Kilreany, not far from Clonard, and opened his school-books. Aged fourteen, he should have been at school but, with the outbreak of the Rebellion, this was no longer possible. One morning at the beginning of May a band of rebels, commanded by a man called Casey, had attacked the Protestant charter-school in Carberry, five miles away, as well as a number of Protestant houses. It was said that some employees of the Grand Canal Company, who were also yeomen, had stored their weapons in the schoolhouse for safe-keeping, and that the rebels were trying to get them. The master, who lived in the schoolhouse, had fought them off with the help of some friends. However, not a day passed but word came of some other outrage, the roads in the area were no longer safe, and so it was now a case of having to study at home.

There had been an arrangement that the master would call to Kilreany and give George some private tuition, but that had become very irregular due to the Rebellion. The net result was that, for the most part, he was left to his own devices.

It was a move which, if the truth be known, George greatly welcomed. His older brothers, Adam who was almost eighteen and Thomas who was sixteen, were inclined to tease him about having to study. They were old enough to be exempt from studies and left each day to take up duty in the Sheriff's House at Clonard, a heavily fortified building which was used to guard an important bridge across the River Boyne. However, he didn't mind their taunts. After all, there were compensations.

Although George's father, Lieutenant Thomas Tyrell, was High Sheriff of Kildare and lived at Kilreany, it was the house at Clonard with its high protective boundary wall that was known as the Sheriff's House. Lieutenant Tyrell was in charge of the garrison there and was always busy, making sure the sentries were keeping an eye on the bridge or, when the occasion demanded it, sallying forth to chase rebels. George's mother, on the other hand, was kept busy trying to run both houses, for although they were only about two miles apart, many of the staff had deserted them.

Situated on rising ground, Kilreany House commanded a fine view of the surrounding countryside. Now, as George looked out of the drawing-room window, he could see that the fields were bathed in sunshine. July was just around the corner and he was thinking of nipping out to the gardens to see if there might be anything worth picking, when he spotted a rider in a dark-blue tunic galloping up the driveway. Realising that it was his father, he raced out to the front steps just as the horse came skidding to a halt in a shower of gravel.

'George,' his father shouted. 'Get the chaise ready, I want you to take your mother to Clonard and give a message to your brothers. Hurry.'

Wondering what was up, George sprinted round to the back yard. There, with the help of a stable-boy who had remained loyal to them, he pulled out the four-wheeled carriage which they called the chaise and yoked up two horses to it, one on either side of the single shaft. Because the carriage had a closed-in cab with a platform in front for luggage, the driver had to ride one of the horses. This was always the one on the left, and George chose his mother's mare, Veritas, as the driver's mount, as she was steady and reliable.

'Now George,' said his father, when he had drawn the carriage up at the front door. 'When you get to Clonard, tell them that a large body of rebels has taken up position

on Fox's Hill. Tell them to send word to Major John
Ormsby in Edenderry. Ask him to despatch as many
troops as he can.'

George could see that his father had removed his
helmet and was sweating profusely from the excitement
and the exertion of the ride.

'I don't know what their intentions are,' he went on,
'but they're too close to the house for comfort. So I'm
sending your mother over to Clonard with you until the
danger passes. Drive hard and don't stop for anyone.' He
handed George one of his pistols, adding, 'Not for anyone now, do you hear?'

George nodded and pushed the pistol into his belt. As
his father gave him a leg up on to Veritas, he asked, 'And
what are you going to do?'

His father was now helping his mother into the cab,
and when he had closed the door, he replied, 'I'm going
to cut across country to Kinnegad and get the troops that
are quartered there.'

Taking the reins firmly in both hands, George waited
until his father had mounted his own horse. Then he
spurred Veritas into action and off they went. A few
moments later, the wheels of the carriage skidded around
the gate-post and, with the firmness of the road now
underneath, he urged the horses on to even greater speed.
At he same time he could see his father riding across the
fields, his helmet firmly back on his head, intent on
getting to Kinnegad as quickly as possible.

Even though it was only a short distance to Clonard,
the road was narrow and had more twists and turns than
George could ever remember. As he rounded one of these
he suddenly found his way blocked by two rebels on
horseback and had to pull savagely on the reins to avoid a
collision. To make matters worse, one of the rebels fired a
pistol in the air. Both of the carriage horses reared up,
whinnying with fright, and the chaise slewed dangerously
to one side.

Glancing back, George could see his mother peering anxiously out of the front window. For a moment he was tempted to grab his father's pistol and fire at the rebels, but it was all he could do to hold on to the reins. Both horses were highly agitated. They continued to prance and rear up and there were moments when, it seemed, the carriage was going to overturn. However, George was also aware that their prancing prevented the rebels from either grabbing them by the halter or taking a shot at him or his mother.

Realising this themselves, the rebels backed off for a moment, enabling the horses to be brought under control. Seizing his opportunity, George shouted, 'Hold on, mother' and, with loud shouts of encouragement, urged the horses forward. Excited as they were, both horses sprang into action, forcing the rebels to scatter into the ditches on either side.

As the carriage bounced along the twisting road George used the reins freely to whip the horses on and didn't stop until they reached the Sheriff's House. Unknown to him, a look-out in one of the stone turrets on the boundary wall had seen the confrontation. He now fired his musket in the direction of the rebels to discourage them from giving pursuit and called on the sentries to open the gates. A few minutes later the carriage careered into the courtyard, George pulled the horses to a halt and the heavy wooden gates closed behind them.

As several members of the garrison grabbed the horses by the halter and tried to calm them down, George slipped to the ground and ran back to help his mother from the carriage. Adam and Thomas were there now too and, as soon as he gave them the message, a member of the cavalry, who was already mounted for some other purpose, was directed to ride with all possible haste to Edenderry and give the message to Major Ormsby.

The following day, 30 June, George watched from one of the turrets of the Sheriff's House as his father joined

Major Ormsby and rode out at the head of a small force
of troops to join battle with the rebels who had gathered
at Fox's Hill. It was an anxious wait for him and his
mother and indeed for all who were left behind.
Eventually, word arrived that the rebels had been routed,
but it wasn't until the evening of 1 July, when George's
father and a number of other officers had gathered in the
Sheriff's House that he realised they had scored a great
victory.

The battle had taken place on the very same day that
Colonel Holt and his men had scored their great victory
over the Ancient Britons at Ballyellis. And, just as
Colonel Holt's victory had been celebrated by Tom Howlett's family and their friends, Lieutenant Tyrell's victory
was celebrated by George's family and their friends. But
instead of whiskey, it was glasses of champagne that were
raised, and instead of *Erin go Bragh,* the toast was God
Save the King.

Although it was Lieutenant Tyrell who had organised
the attack, it was Major Ormsby who had led it and he
was in a particularly happy mood. When the champagne
had taken effect and he and the other officers had
discarded their tunics, he produced a letter which he said
he was sending to the Chief Secretary, Lord Castlereagh.

George and his brothers listened, fascinated, as the
major described in his letter how the rebels, who were
about three hundred strong, had retreated into a bog.

'I pursued them and they fled, keeping up a smart fire
on us in every direction,' he read. 'However, I soon
routed them out of the bog and killed a number of them
and they were cut to pieces in every direction out of the
bog, which was by this time completely surrounded. The
numbers killed, I can't tell, but from every account I
should suppose not less than a hundred must have been
killed and wounded.'

George's cousin, Richard Allen, who was a member of
the garrison at the Sheriff's House raised his glass, saying,

'A great victory, Sir. A great victory. And your losses?'

Major Ormsby turned to the second page of his letter and, by way of answer, continued, 'I have the pleasure to inform your Lordship that we only lost two horses which were killed by a Captain Casey and six of the rebels who got out of the bog. They were all killed and as Casey belonged to this town – that's Edenderry – we brought him in and hung him up where he now remains.'

At this news a great cheer went up, but George didn't join in. He was wondering if it was the same Casey who had attacked the schoolhouse and had mixed feelings about it as he didn't like school.

Major Ormsby then went on to list all the officers, including Lieutenant Tyrell, who had taken part in the action. There were smiles and nods all round as the names were read out, and one of the officers lifted his glass, saying, 'God Save the King.' The others lifted their glasses, and repeated, 'God Save the King.'

'And here's to the Battle of Fox's Hill,' said the same officer. Once again the others lifted their glasses to join in the toast, adding, 'To the Battle of Fox's Hill.'

In case the rebels might plan a revenge attack on Kilreany House, George's father decided that they should move out of it altogether and take up residence in the Sheriff's House. It was now approaching the Twelfth of July when loyalists would celebrate the Battle of the Boyne. Little did George and his family know that it was the Sheriff's House that would be attacked, and that they would soon be involved in their own battle of the Boyne.

Colonel Holt mounted up, gave orders for his colours to be hoisted, and set off at the head of his men. Carried aloft for all to see, his flag fluttered and unfurled in the evening breeze. It was green and, when caught by the rays of the setting sun or a change in the breeze, was seen have the two letters JH in yellow on one side, and an uncrowned harp on the other.

The rest of the leaders were on the move now too, some in front of him, some behind, and each flying his own distinctive flag. Each of the contingents that followed them also carried flags. Some of these were green, some white, and many bore emblems of the harp was well as the words *Erin go Bragh*. Here and there, other larger flags fluttered above the heads of the marchers, many of whom were armed with pikes and muskets. And waving them good-bye were groups of women and children who would pray, not only for their safe return, but for the day when they could all return to their homes.

To Tom Howlett, who watched from a nearby hill with Antrim John, it looked as if a colony of ants was swarming out of the camp. Thanks to the northerner, Tom had got Betsy back and was now sitting on a comfortable saddle which his friend had also procured for him. If only, he thought, his mother and father could see him now, for he also had a pair of pistols in his belt which Colonel Holt had given to him for his own protection.

In the excitement of the moment, it never occurred to Tom that his parents would have been very worried for his safety; nor indeed did it occur to him that such a great army could ever be defeated. For in spite of Colonel Holt's reservations about the proposal to march on the Sheriff's House, it seemed to Tom that the rebel army must be invincible.

So vast were the numbers now on the move that the news that many rebels had surrendered following recent defeats in Wexford paled into insignificance. Large numbers, it was reported, had availed of amnesty terms introduced by the new Viceroy, Lord Cornwallis. This, Tom was told, meant that, weary of fighting, they had accepted pardons. Perhaps this was why the Wexfordmen who had marched to Whelp Rock had done so with even greater determination to fight on. Now as Tom watched them setting off, he tried to see if he could spot the green pennant of the Whitechurch contingent, for it was so long

The rebel army leaves Whelp Rock

he couldn't help wondering if it was being carried by someone on foot or on horseback. But there were too many people, too many flags, and the light was fading fast.

'Come on, Tom boy,' said Antrim John, 'Time we caught up with them.'

Soon the twilight of the summer night closed in around the rebel army, obscuring them with a mantle of darkness from those who might be watching from afar, yet giving them enough light to find their way down into the lowlands. There they collected carts and provisions which had been stored away in advance and, after a short rest, resumed their march in the early morning.

For the first time, Tom now had a great feeling of adventure, a feeling of belonging to a great conquering mass of people. And, even though Colonel Holt had spoken against the expedition, he was chosen to lead it. This, Tom learned, wasn't because he was senior to any of the other officers; indeed, there were some, such as Anthony Perry, who were regarded as being more senior than he was. It was simply because he knew the roads in the area better than anyone else.

'Once,' he told Tom as they rode along together, 'I travelled the length and breadth of Leinster. That was when I was employed to grade woollen goods produced in the cottages. I also worked at one time as an overseer on the construction of roads. But then, I've held a number of jobs.'

'What like?' asked Tom.

'Well, in my early days I worked on a farm, you know, as a gamekeeper, things like that. Then I went to the north of Ireland to improve myself in farming. On my return to Dublin, I was prevailed upon to join the 32nd Regiment of Foot as a recruiting officer.' He smiled and added, 'I was a good recruiting officer too. In the course of twenty-one days I obtained thirty-two recruits. But I only stayed in the army for a little while. My parents prevailed upon me to give it up.'

'Then what did you do?' asked Tom.

Colonel Holt smiled again and told him, 'I got married to my wife, Hester, up in Roundwood. And then I be-came a billet-master.'

'What's that?'

'My job was to find accommodation in local houses for members of the Antrim Militia, which I did. I even had some of them in my own house. But then I was accused of trying to recruit some of them for the United Irishmen, and they burned my house down.'

'And is it true that you captured Rogers the robber?'

Colonel Holt nodded. 'Him and several more of his gang. And, I might add, without fee or reward.'

'Why then did you go after them?' asked Tom.

'Because,' he replied, 'I hate thieves and robbers, that's why.'

They had now left the mountains behind and were out in the open. Before them lay the rolling fields of Kildare and Colonel Holt sent out his best horsemen to scout the area. This, he told Tom, was where they were most vul-nerable. Great and all as their numbers were, he reckoned that if they were taken by surprise they would never even reach Clonard.

8

The Lion and the King

As the stage-coach pulled in at the toll-house beside the bridge, George Tyrell ran out to meet it. The driver, he knew, would stop only long enough to pay the toll for using the road, then he would drive into the yard of the inn on the far side of the bridge to change the horses.

Up in one of the stone turrets of the Sheriff's House a sentry rested the long barrel of his musket on the ledge of a square peep-hole and watched. Like the rest of the garrison, he had been told to keep an eye on the boy and make sure he didn't come to any harm.

Running after the coach, George pulled himself up and swung out of the back of it until it stopped at the inn. There he watched the passengers disembark and waited to see how many of them would read the sign above the door. Some of them did stop to read it, and a few smiled when they did so. For the sign said, 'Good Dry Lodgings. And breakfast by Hug Enis Clenard.' Only people of some education, George reckoned, would notice the stonemason's spelling mistakes. And their smiles would come from the fact that the mason had run out of space, forcing him to put the 'h' above the 'g' to make it Hugh.

George's game, and one he often played, was to try and figure out what type of people the passengers might be. A big raw-boned man who carried a bit of a stick and paid little attention to the sign might, he reckoned, not be able to read. He might be a dealer in horses or cattle, a person with a good eye and a strong hand for striking a bargain, but with little or no education. A portly man who would look at the sign and not smile might be a businessman of limited education who could read but was too busy to smile. On the other hand, a man who looked at the sign and smiled was obviously a person of some education who could not only read but had time to see the humorous side of life. If he carried a leather bag, he might be a physician, or, if he had a walking cane, he might be a man of leisure, a member, even, of a big house... And so the guessing game went on.

Whether or not they understood what the sign said, the passengers finished their drinks as soon as the horses were changed and climbed back into the coach. With the country in such a state of unrest they were obviously anxious to get to their destination as quickly as possible.

George waited until the coach had disappeared in a cloud of dust, then wandered back to the bridge. He liked to be out and about but there was no one to play with, so he leaned over the parapet and scanned the dark waters of the River Boyne for any sign of fish. The sky was blue with only a few white clouds and he could feel the heat of the sun on the back of his neck. Up along the river, the fronds of elderberry had almost lost their whiteness and the insects that fed upon them had turned to the blossoms on the brambles in their search for nourishment.

In the fields beyond the river, George could see that while the local population had been in a state of rebellion, the corn had been ripening in the sun – would it ever be harvested and the grain brought to his uncle's mill? Going over to the other parapet he picked up a small yellow and brown snail shell. It was empty and he wondered if the snail that had occupied it had been devoured by the ants that were busy coming and going in the crevices above.

Pocketing the shell, George returned to the house. There he collected his school-books from the bedroom that had been assigned to him, and made his way reluctantly downstairs to resume his studies. Looking up at the Tyrell coat of arms above the massive open fireplace, he couldn't help wondering if their house at Kilreany was still standing, or if the rebels had set fire to it as they had done to so many other big houses. The same coat of arms adorned the walls at Kilreany and, since his childhood, he had been told many stories about what the various emblems meant.

The Tyrells, he knew, could trace their roots back centuries, even, it was said, to a time before Christ. They has served many kings and many causes, coming to England with William the Conqueror and paving the way for Strongbow to come to Ireland. At least six of the crosses on the coat of arms, he had been told, could be traced to members of the family who had taken part in the third crusade to the Holy Land.

It had always fascinated George to think that some of his ancestors had been crusaders, riding off with the Kings of England to liberate Jerusalem from the Turks and deliver it into the hands of the Christians. However, it was the story of the lion on the coat of arms that had intrigued him most, for the back legs and hind quarters were missing. According to tradition, there had been a full lion on the coat of arms of Sir Walter Tyrell the third, but it had been cut in two after he had been blamed for killing the Red King.

George smiled as he thought of the numerous times he had asked his mother to tell him the story at bedtime. William the Red, she had always reminded him, was the son of William the Conqueror and was known as the Red King, or Rufus, because of the colour of his hair.

'It was a long time ago,' his mother always began, settling herself on the edge of the large four-poster bed, 'in the year 1100 to be exact. One day Rufus and his brother, Fine-scholar, and some friends, went to the New Forest to hunt deer. Rufus and Fine-scholar had fallen out after the death of their father, but now they were reconciled. They stayed in a hunting-lodge where, it is said, there was a good deal of merry-making before they retired for the night. Next morning, before the party split up and the hounds were set loose, a blacksmith brought six bolts or arrows of superior workmanship as an offering to Rufus. The king then presented two of the arrows to Sir Walter, saying – in French, of course, for they were Normans, *"Bon archer, bonnes flèches,"* meaning, a good archer, good arrows.'

Sir Walter, his mother always explained, was a famous sportsman and, when the party split up, he was the only one the king took with him. That was the last time anyone saw the king alive. As evening approached a poor charcoal-burner, passing through the forest with his cart, came upon his body. He had been shot with an arrow in the chest and his clothes and red beard were clotted with blood. Suspicion immediately fell on Sir Walter, so he fled to Normandy where he claimed the protection of the King of France.

'And did he really kill Rufus?' George would ask.

'I don't believe he did,' his mother would always reply. 'At least not intentionally. I suppose it all depends on which story you believe. According to the first one Sir Walter and the king had taken up positions on opposite sides of a covert when a stag appeared. The king's bowstring broke and he called out, in French again, of course, "Tirez donc, Gautier, tirez donc, si meme c'etait le diable!" meaning, "Go ahead, shoot, Walter, shoot in the devil's name." Walter then fired, but the arrow glanced off a tree. He was unaware that the arrow had struck the king until he went to recover it and found Rufus mortally wounded.'

'And what did Sir Walter say happened?' George would ask.

'Well,' his mother would continue, 'According to the second story, Walter denied that he killed the king. It's said that he returned to England and showed King Henry the arrows he got from Rufus, thus proving that the one found in the King's body could not have been fired by him. Henry pardoned him, but to mark his displeasure at his flight to France, he cut the lion in his arms in two. However, he then eased the punishment by giving him the motto, *Veritas via Vitae.'*

George would smile and, having been told so often
what the motto meant, add, 'Truth is the way of life.'
Then, before he dozed off, he would asked, 'So who did
kill the king?'

'Well,' his mother would whisper, 'there was another
story. That was that at breakfast on the morning of the
hunt, the King also gave two arrows to someone else and
that maybe the King's brother caused him to be killed.
Who knows?'

George's mother had a name for the other member of
the hunting party, but he was always asleep by the time
she got to the end of the story and could never remember
who it was. Even now, as he looked up at the lion, he
thought how much he loved the story. Wrenching his eyes
from the crest, he forced himself to do the studies his
mother had now instructed him to do. Much more to his
liking was the firing practice he and his brothers were to
get after lunch. He just hoped that if an attack did come,
his aim would be true and, unlike Sir Walter, he would
find his mark.

Because Tom Howlett had been seen so much in the
company of Colonel Holt many of those who were
marching to Clonard believed they were father and son.
There was also another reason for this belief, as Tom
discovered when a young rebel pulled his horse up beside
him.

Having introduced himself as Captain Farrell, the
young man inquired if Tom was Colonel Holt's son. On
being told that this was not the case, he expressed
surprise, saying, 'But the name's the same.'

Tom shook his head. 'No, my name's Howlett.'

'Howlt–Howlett. Seems all the same to me,' said the
young man.

Tom smiled. He knew that in their own country way of
pronouncing the name, many of the rebels spoke of
Colonel Howlt rather than Holt. 'The names might

sound the same,' he explained, 'but they're not.'

The young men smiled and, raising his eyebrows in a way that suggested he was still a little perplexed, nodded. At the same time he gave Tom a little salute to show that whether or not he was the leader's son, he was still someone who was close to him and deserved respect.

O I wanted to ask Captain Farrell where he was from, Tom wrote in his journal, but he galloped off before I could do so. The next time I saw him he was leading the charge on the Sheriff's House at Clonard and I never discovered where he was from. In any event, I now had other, more serious things, to occupy my mind. We were out in the open and, after what Colonel Joe had said about being vulnerable, I feared that we would be attacked at any moment. Apart from our great numbers, our activities could not but draw attention to our passage through Kildare. Our outriders were continually seizing horses so that as many as possible of our members could be mounted and, as we had to live off the countryside, raiding parties were taking cattle, poultry and anything else they could lay their hands on.

News that a contingent of yeomen were shadowing us added to my fears, but Antrim John assured me that I had nothing to worry about. Some of our best horsemen, he informed me, were ranging far and wide to make sure no one launched a surprise attack on us. At the same time, the musketeers and pikemen were keeping to the roads. By doing so, he explained, they could use the high hedges as cover and repel attack from either side, while carts and cattle were being kept at the front and rear to serve as barricades for the musketeers should attacks come from there. Shortly after that I learned that Colonel Joe had sent out two hundred horsemen to drive the yeomen off, but still, I worried. Few, if any rebels, were rushing to join us along the way. Indeed, it seemed to me that our numbers were diminishing rather than increasing. Many were suffering from fatigue and I suspected that a goodly number were slipping away each night.

I also knew from what was being said that gunpowder and ammunition were in short supply. On reaching Kilcullen we were told that a small party of soldiers had just passed through with a keg of gunpowder. A party of mounted men immediately set off in pursuit of them and returned a short time later with the barrel. It was smaller than expected but such was the situation that it was considered a welcome addition to our supplies.

To me this episode in itself seemed to underline our perilous position, and I asked Antrim John what would happen if the King's troops attacked us in force? Surely, I told him, they could not be in ignorance of where we were. However, Antrim John didn't seem too concerned. He reckoned that the troops who had dispersed the Wexfordmen were probably searching for them in the mountains of south Wicklow, while the military who were stationed in Dublin would stay there rather than leave it unprotected. As for the garrisons in the small villages and towns, they would sit tight and see what was going to happen.

At the village of Kill some of the rebels held up the mail-coach and destroyed it. Why they did so, I do not know. Somehow I suspect that they looked upon it as a symbol of Government and burned it, either to disrupt the mail or demonstrate that the Government's writ no longer ran in Kildare. In any event, we pushed on and later that day made contact with the Kildare rebels who were hiding out in Timahoe Bog. However, at a meeting in the nearby village of Prosperous, their leader, William Aylmer, told our leaders that there were fewer rebels in the area than they might have expected and that some of them were not prepared to join in the attack on Clonard.

This news was received with great disappointment, but it was decided that there could be no turning back. So we kept going and didn't stop until we pitched camp a few miles from Clonard. It was now the evening of 10 July. The attack on the Sheriff's House, I learned, was to be launched the next morning. Before I retired for the night, I heard various officers reporting on their numbers and state of readiness. When the numbers were added up, it was Colonel Joe's reckoning that about two and a half thousand had deserted since we had left Whelp Rock. It was, therefore, with the greatest forebodings that I lay down in my tent and tried to go to sleep.

At what time I drifted off, I do not know, but I dreamt that I was back in my home in the Avoca valley and that my father was once again reading about the four beasts from the Book of Revelations. Only it wasn't his voice I was hearing, but a voice that sounded as if it were coming from heaven. The lion was inviting me to come and see, and I saw a white horse. 'And he that sat on him,' the voice was saying, 'had a bow, and a crown was given unto him, and he went forth conquering and to conquer.'

In desperation, I looked at the conquering figure on the white horse to see if it was Colonel Joe, but it wasn't. Then another beast invited me to come and see, and I saw a red horse. 'And power was given to him that sat thereon,' the voice was saying, 'to take peace from the earth, and there was given unto him a great sword...'

The second beast was the calf, and now I could see the figure on the red horse riding across the countryside, sword in hand, driving a herd of cattle before him. There was blood on the sword, and I could see quite clearly that the figure was that of Colonel Joe.

When I awoke it was early morning. Colonel Joe had already buckled on his silver-mounted sword and was busy marshalling his men. It was 11 July. The attack on the Sheriff's House at Clonard was about to begin. First, however, Colonel Joe asked Antrim John and myself to scout the area and 'see if the coast was clear'. O

9

The Meeting

It was now ten days since the rebels had been driven from Fox's Hill and Mrs Tyrell insisted on going back to Kilreany to make sure the house there was still intact. Standing in the courtyard of the Sheriff's House, she watched as the two horses were yoked up to the shaft of her carriage and, when George and his brothers had helped to fasten the harness, she climbed into the cab. The driver was given a leg up on to Veritas and off they went. George followed at a trot until they had driven out through the gates and watched as they set off at a smart pace down the narrow road that ran beside the high, stone boundary wall. Being an accomplished horsewoman herself and a person of strong and independent mind, Mrs Tyrell had brushed aside any suggestion that it might be dangerous to leave the Sheriff's House, or that anyone, other than the driver, should go with her.

Seeing that his father was busy organising members of the garrison for their daily guard duties, George, free of parental authority, headed down the dusty road to a tall grey building, at the side of which was a large wooden water-wheel. Situated a short distance on the Dublin side of the Sheriff's House, this was his uncle John's flour mill. Built in 1793, it took in grain from an area that stretched far beyond the boundaries of Kildare and Meath.

Whether it was because his Uncle John was in England, or because of the Rebellion, George didn't know, but the mill was deserted. Like the water-wheel, the huge cogged wheels and grinding stones that reduced the grain to flour inside the mill were at a standstill. The workers had gone, either because there was no work or because they feared the wrath of the rebels if they continued to work for people who were the symbol of authority in Kildare.

Having no fewer than four lofts, the mill was one of the highest in the area, higher even than the Norman mound that was situated just inside the gates of the Sheriff's House. There were no windows in the top loft, apart from skylights, and, making his way to the one below it, George looked out across the countryside to the left. His mother's carriage had already disappeared into the maze of hedgerows and winding roads that led to Kilreany. There was no other activity that would suggest the presence of rebels and he switched to windows over-looking the main road to see if there was any sign of the stage-coach from Dublin.

Trees that George's uncle had planted in a field beside the mill weren't yet tall enough to obscure the view, and he could see the road clearly in both directions. There was no sign of the coach, and he wondered if the service had been cancelled because of news that the mail-coach had been destroyed by rebels at Kill the previous day. In fact, the only movement he could see on the road was a tall red-haired man who was walking down towards the Sheriff's House. Even the cabins in the vicinity of the mill seemed deserted; everyone seemed to have gone.

George was turning to go when, to his surprise, he found himself face to face with another boy. 'Who are you?' he demanded. 'And what are you doing here?'

Tom Howlett had been told to wait at the mill while Antrim John had a closer look at the Sheriff's House and, being the son of a miller, he had gone upstairs to have a look around. Now, he was equally startled to find another boy there and, when asked to explain his presence, could only reply, 'Nothing.'

'What do you mean, nothing?' George asked him. 'This is private property. You've no right to be here.'

'I'm sorry,' said Tom, regaining his composure. 'It's just that my father owns a mill and I was curious to see what this one was like.'

'Where?'

Tom startles George Tyrell at the mill

'Well, it's only a small mill, not nearly as big as this. It's in the Avoca valley.'

'And what are you doing up here?'

From the way George spoke, Tom realised from the outset that he was a member of an upper-class family, the kind of family that would be serving king and country. So he said, 'There's a lot of trouble down in Wicklow. You know, with the Rebellion and all. My parents thought it would be safer if I went to stay with my aunt in Mullingar.'

'You mean on your own?'

Tom shook his head. 'No. One of my father's workers is with me. He's gone down to the bridge to make sure the road is clear of rebels.'

George looked out of the window again, but the red-haired man had disappeared.

'Is this your father's mill?' Tom asked him.

George turned to face him. 'No, it's my uncle's.'

Tom nodded, and going over to the window looked down. Now, for the first time, he could see the Sheriff's House in its entirety. Besides the mansion itself, there were many other buildings and all were completely enclosed by a high boundary wall. 'What a house!' he exclaimed. 'Is that yours?'

George could see that Tom was a boy of some education and found his story that he was the son of a miller quite plausible. However, he also knew that some merchants were involved with the rebels, so he just said, 'It's the Sheriff's House.'

'And look at the flags,' said Tom.

'They're the flags of the Kildare Militia,' George told him. 'The one with red, white and blue, that's the King's Colour. The other one, the black one, that's the regimental flag.'

George's familiarity with the flags confirmed Tom's view that he had come from a big house, possibly even the Sheriff's House. Seeing red-coated soldiers spreading across the courtyard, he asked, 'What are they doing?'

George knew that the members of the garrison were heading for the turrets and other look-out posts around the wall to relieve those who had been on duty during the night, but he just said, 'They're guarding the bridge.'

'What would happen if the rebels got in here?' Tom asked. 'Would they not be able to fire down on them?'

Once George had asked his father the same question, only to be told that test firings had shown the mill to be too far away. So he shook his head, saying, 'They're out of range.'

As Tom continued to view the Sheriff's House, George said, 'Look. We'd better go. We're not really supposed to be here.'

Turning away from the window, Tom nodded. 'Anyway, I have to be on my way.'

For a moment the two boys looked at one another, each wondering who the other really was. Perhaps the thought crossed their minds that they might become friends. But if it did, instinct told them it wasn't to be. And so, on the road outside, they went their separate ways, Tom in search of Antrim John, George in search of his father who had promised to allow him to do some sentry duty.

Having made their way back to the rebel camp, Tom and Antrim John reported to Colonel Joe.

'It's like a fort,' Antrim John told him. 'There's a high wall all around it.'

'That's right,' said Tom. 'I saw it from the mill. There are soldiers inside and sentry-posts along the walls.'

'Could we use the mill?' asked Colonel Joe. 'I mean, to fire on them?'

Tom shook his head. 'I don't think so. It's too far away.'

Colonel Joe frowned. 'Without artillery, it's going to be difficult to get in.' He took a deep breath. 'Well, there's no going back now. I'll brief the others. Then we attack.'

10

The Moment of Truth

Because George's brothers were old enough to be members of the Kildare Militia, they now wore the regiment's uniform. This consisted of a scarlet tunic and white breeches, but for identification purposes each regiment had collars, cuffs and lapels of a different colour. In the case of the Kildare militia, the key colour was black, and the two older boys now affected superiority over their younger brother by plucking at their black cuffs and collars in a way that upper-class gentlemen were inclined to do.

However, the long-barrelled musket that had just been issued to George was the only symbol of military membership or acceptance that he required. By this stage he had been trained how to use it and he now proceeded to demonstrate his expertise. He had also been issued with a pouch of cartridges, each of which consisted of a lead ball and the right amount of powder to fire it, both wrapped together in paper. Ignoring his brothers' affectations, he stood the musket on its butt and proceeded to load it. Taking a cartridge from the pouch, he bit off the end of the paper and poured the powder into the barrel. Then he squeezed the paper around the ball so that it would fit tightly in the barrel and rammed it down on top of the powder.

While his brothers were still pretending that they weren't really interested in what he was doing, George knew that they were watching his every move so that they could poke fun at him if he made a mistake.

Having put the ramrod back in its place beneath the barrel, he took up the musket and checked the flint-lock to make sure it was at the safety position of half-cock. He then poured some finer powder into the small cup-shaped priming-pan above the trigger and put the cover over it to make sure it didn't blow away. He knew from what his instructor had told him that when the flint sent a spark into the pan, the flash would go into the barrel through the small touchhole beside it, thus igniting the powder inside and causing the gun to fire the ball.

Not having spotted any mistakes in his loading procedure, George's brothers now began to tease him. Adam was telling him that he couldn't hit a barn door when there were shouts of alarm from the sentries up on the walls. A few moments later a member of the yeomanry corps galloped into the yard. As the rider dismounted, George could see it was their cousin, Richard Allen. His horse was in a lather of sweat and he wasn't much better, shouting that he had been pursued by a large party of rebels and that he was sure they were advancing on Clonard.

'I was almost taken myself,' he informed his uncle, who had just rushed out of the house to see what all the commotion was about.

Lieutenant Tyrell immediately ordered the gates to be closed, issued an ample supply of cartridges to all members of the garrison and directed them to take up duty at various points. Marksmen were placed at the windows of the big house, while others were despatched to firing positions around the boundary wall. Young and all as he was, George was also pressed into duty, and almost before he knew what was happening, found himself in a turret in the garden with six yeomen, including his cousin Richard.

The turret had a commanding view of the approach roads and the bridge. Pushing the barrel of his musket out through one of the firing-holes, George was mesmerised to see a large number of rebels on horseback. They were coming along the road towards him and, beyond them, a multitude of others were coming through the fields on foot. How, he wondered, could the garrison possibly repel so many? On the window-sill beside the barrel was the small brown snail shell he had picked up on the bridge. He must have left it there when playing in the turret, he thought, and he wondered if, like the ants that had cleared out the shell, the rebels would overcome them and clear out the Sheriff's House. As rebel activity in the area had increased, his father, he knew, had asked Lord Castlereagh to send him reinforcements, only to be told that arms and ammunition he could have in plenty, but no troops. His father had then recruited and armed nineteen local Protestants, but, even so, George knew that the garrison now numbered only twenty-eight, and that included himself and his brothers.

George was now training the barrel of his musket on the leading rider, but he held his fire as he reckoned the rider was still out of range. He waited, then slowly pulled back the flint-lock to full-cock and squeezed the trigger. There was a flash followed by a deafening report and the rider fell from his horse. Almost immediately, a shot from one of the rebels ricocheted off the sill, taking the snail shell with it and leaving only a dent in the stone where the shell had been. As George withdrew to reload, his cousin Richard took his place. A general volley of shots from the garrison followed and, taken by surprise, the rebel horsemen withdrew out of range. Although he didn't know it yet, the youngest member of the Tyrell family had killed the first rebel in what would become known as the battle of Clonard.

From the safety of a nearby rise, Tom Howlett sat on his mare and watched the rebel force surround the Sheriff's House. When Antrim John had been assigned to other duties he had hoped that young Captain Farrell might have been given the job of keeping an eye on him. However, he had learned that Farrell had been chosen to lead the charge on the Sheriff's House and another rebel, a much older man, was told to look after him.

Betsy was at an age when very little disturbed her and, while a younger horse might have become excited with all the comings and goings, she barely moved, except to twitch an ear or flick her tail when a horse-fly pierced her skin. Her young rider was less composed and, when the first shot from the garrison swept Captain Farrell from his mount, Tom cried out in a mixture of shock and sadness. He had only met the young rebel for a few minutes, but somehow he felt he had known him all his life.

Seeing Tom's distress and, knowing from experience that the death of Captain Farrell would be the first of many, the older man took Betsy by the bridle and led her around the back of the besieging rebel force to the relative safety of the mill. There, in the trees, he dismounted and helped Tom to the ground.

At the foot of the stairs they met several other rebels who had hoped to use the mill to fire down on the Sheriff's House, but had found it out of range. Climbing the stairs to the loft where Tom had met the other boy earlier that morning, they hurried over to the windows and anxiously scanned the battle scene.

From what he had heard of their plan, Tom knew that while the rebels on horseback were launching their attack Colonel Holt, Garret Byrne, Edward Fitzgerald, and a contingent of musketmen had been hoping to surprise the garrison from the rear. Instead, it seemed, the musketmen had been surprised, and some of them had been cut down in a withering volley of shots from the garrison.

A short time later, smoke began to billow up from the direction of the bridge and, before it obscured his view, Tom could see other rebels creeping along beneath the boundary wall of the house, while here and there some had gained a vantage point of rising ground and were exchanging fire with the garrison.

Unable to see anything more because of the smoke, Tom and his minder made their way back to the rise from which they had seen the battle begin. Along the hedgerows and ditches, they came across hundreds of musketmen waiting their turn to join in the attack.

'Why don't they join in now?' Tom asked his companion.

'Well,' said the older man, 'I'd say the leaders don't want to commit all of their men at the same time. You see, many will die, and many will run out of powder or ball. Then it'll be the turn of these men.'

Further back still, Tom discovered that large numbers of pikemen were lying in the ditches. Leaning against the grassy banks, they gripped their long-handled pikes and, like the forward lines of musketmen, waited anxiously for the moment when they would be ordered to attack. However, it was apparent, even to Tom's inexperienced eye, that there was little they could do. Nor, indeed, was there much the musketmen could do. Not only did the garrison have the advantage of firing down from the house and its walls; they also had the protection that these afforded. It was also becoming obvious that they had an unlimited supply of ammunition.

Rebels who had been slightly wounded or who had run out of ammunition were now coming back and the news they brought with them tended to confirm that it was an uphill battle.

'How is it going?' they were asked.

'Not so good,' they invariably replied.

Colonel Holt, they said, had set fire to two small cabins near the bridge to give them cover. Even then, he had lost eight or nine more men. Now he had switched his attack to the front gates and sent for loads of straw. When the gates were forced open, he would try and burn the garrison out of the turret in the garden.

Hearing this, Tom realised how right Colonel Holt had been. Without heavy guns it was going to be difficult, if not impossible, to dislodge the musketeers who were defending the Sheriff's House.

11

Odd One Out

Having deployed his best marksmen at vantage points in and around the Sheriff's House, Lieutenant Tyrell directed several others to go to the magazine where the cartridges were kept and keep the musketeers well supplied. There were, he reckoned, thousands of rebels now laying siege to the house, but it appeared to him that they were poorly armed. Lord Castlereagh, on the other hand, had sent him a plentiful supply of guns and ammunition.

Seeing the rebels mount what appeared to be a guard on the bridge across the River Boyne, the marksmen at the windows opened fire, killing about a dozen of them and dispersing the rest. It was to guard this bridge that the Sheriff's House had been built, and they knew it must be kept open if there was to be any hope of rescue. In the turret in the garden, young George Tyrell and his cousin, Richard Allen, were in a much more confined space than those in the house and finding conditions almost unbearable. The battle had been in progress for several hours now and they were sweating, not only from the heat of the day, but from the exertion of loading and reloading their muskets. The acrid smell of gunsmoke was also filling the turret, choking them and burning their eyes so that they were firing almost blindly from the peep-holes.

To make matters worse, the rebels had set fire to some cabins near the bridge, and smoke from those was also finding its way into the turret. There was, however, no time to feel sorry for themselves. Some of the rebels had now forced open the front gates and were rushing towards the turret.

'Quickly,' shouted Richard, 'pull up the ladder!'

Opening the trapdoor in the floor, two of the yeomen

pulled up the ladder that gave them access to the turret and slammed the door shut just as the first of the rebels arrived beneath them. A volley of shots followed, but the yeomen had stepped back just in time and the musket-balls that came up through the timber floor failed to find their mark.

Not knowing what to expect next, Richard directed George and the yeomen to press themselves back against the walls. A few minutes later, it became obvious that the rebels were trying to prise open the trapdoor by climbing up on one another's shoulders, but as soon as it began to open, they were met by a volley of shots that sent them crashing to the ground.

Incensed by their casualties and their inability to get at the small garrison in the turret, the rebels fired another volley up through the floor. Once again the musket-balls ripped up through the floor and this time they were followed by the blades of pikes as some of the rebels tried to tear the floorboards apart.

More shots were fired down at the attackers and so it went on until one of the yeomen, a local man by the name of Michael Cusack, who was continuing to fire on the rebels at the gates, shouted that they were wheeling in cart-loads of straw. 'I think they're going to try and burn us out,' he warned.

A few minutes later, the firing from below stopped and smoke began to seep up through the floorboards.

'He's right,' whispered George. 'They're trying to burn us out.'

'All right,' said Richard. 'There are only two ways we can get out of here. One is through the trapdoor, the other is through the window. Maybe if we split up, some of us can make it.'

'I'll take my chances with the window,' said one of the yeomen, and several of the others agreed.

'But the window is very high,' said Michael Cusack, who was older and less agile than the rest.

'Right then,' George told him. 'You come with me. We'll take the trapdoor.'

'And I'll go with the others through the window,' said Richard. 'The rebels must be sheltering on the side of the turret away from the house, so we just might make it.'

George nodded. 'With a bit of luck we might get some covering fire from the house.'

The smoke was getting very thick now, and they were beginning to cough. 'All right,' Richard told them, 'let's go – and good luck.'

Dropping through the trapdoor, Richard and Michael Cusack found themselves sliding down through a cart-load of burning straw in such a way that they hit the ground running. Even so, they weren't fast enough. The rebels were waiting for them, and both were hit by musket-balls as they sprinted for the house. However, their injuries weren't serious and they kept running until a few moments later they were pulled in through the front door.

High as the window was, Richard and the other yeomen managed to land without injury and ran to a nearby wall. Using the wall as cover, they eluded the rebels and succeeded in rejoining the rest of the garrison. What neither they nor the rebels knew was that the garrison numbered twenty-seven, not twenty-eight. One member had arrived for guard duty, only to be shut out when the gates were closed against the rebels. In spite of the huge numbers of rebels laying siege to the Sheriff's House, he was now making his way to Kinnegad to raise the alarm.

O The smell of battle was everywhere, Tom Howlet wrote in his journal. Various buildings were now in flames and the smoke from the fires mingled with the more pungent smoke from the muskets so that my eyes smarted. For this small mercy I gave thanks, for those who saw the tears run down my cheeks believed it was the smoke that was making me weep. How could I, on the field of battle, let anyone know I was crying, crying for those who were staggering back with arms and legs that had been cruelly splintered by musket-balls, crying for those who could not walk and lay screaming where they had been shot. The lucky ones, I felt, were those who had been killed, and they were many.

For those whose bones had been shattered, the pain was unbearable, the wounds untreatable. No medical assistance was available, and the crude attempts by their comrades to bind their broken limbs only seemed to make the pain worse. They, I thought, were entitled to cry and, yet, I could not but cry for them, knowing as I did that their pain would end only when consciousness or life itself would end.

It was, therefore, with a great sense of relief and not a little guilt that I was given an excuse to leave the scene. The word was now spreading throughout the rebel forces that the wife of the High Sheriff had been captured and was being held in a house not far distant. Curious to know how this could have happened, and if, indeed, it was true, I prevailed upon my elderly minder to take me there.

By making various inquiries and taking a circuitous route, we came to a cluster of houses where, according to popular opinion, the woman was being held. The place was full of rebels, many of whom, it seemed to me, were more consumed with curiosity about their prisoner than with the battle that was still raging around her home.

Since the account of the woman's capture was on everyone's lips, all we had to do to hear it was stop and listen as it was being told and retold to groups of rebels, many of whom, I suspected, had heard it already. Her carriage, it appears, had been stopped on the road shortly after the attack on the Sheriff's House had begun. Two rebels on horseback had drawn their swords and compelled the driver to turn about.

According to the man who told the story – and, I must

confess, he related it in graphic fashion – the two rebels knew immediately that the woman in the coach must be someone very important, for it was a special type of coach. It was pulled by two horses, and was driven by a servant who rode one of them. Furthermore, it had a coat of arms on the door.

After they had turned around, said the man, they met two hundred men armed with swords, pikes and muskets, some of whom searched the carriage for arms. Three of the rebels then got up and stood on the front of the coach, three others stood on the platform at the back of it and, accompanied by the others, compelled the servant to go with them.

We had no difficulty in finding the coach as a large crowd of rebels had gathered round it, curious to see what it was like and the comfort in which the people in the big house travelled. Squeezing my way through to the front of the crowd, I could see that the two horses were still yoked up to the carriage. The horse on the left had a saddle on its back, but when one of the rebels pulled himself on to it, both horses reared up, throwing him to the ground, They were, I could see, linked to each other by their harness. They were also fairly spirited horses and some of the other rebels were now trying to calm them down.

The coat of arms on the door of the coach featured the top half of a lion, and I couldn't help wondering why they hadn't used the other half. There was also a motto on the crest, but it was in Latin and the little I had learned at school did not enable me to understand it. It was then that I heard someone say that Father Mogue Kearns, who had once served as a curate in the area, had recognised the crest as belonging the High Sheriff, Lieutenant Tyrell. He may also have recognised the woman in the coach as Mrs Tyrell, I do not know. But from what I heard, there were those who had urged that she be treated with the same brutality that many of the United Irishmen had received at the hands of the Crown forces.

Rebels intercept Mrs Tyrell's coach

Others, I'm glad to say, were against this course of action, and Mrs Tyrell was allowed to go into a nearby cottage where two rebels, armed with muskets, were posted to make sure she came to no harm.

It was now mid-afternoon and we knew from the intensity of the shots that the battle for the Sheriff's House was continuing unabated. A pall of black smoke still hung in the blue sky above the battle scene, there being little or no breeze to take it away, and I could not help but wonder if it was high enough to be observed by Crown forces elsewhere in the area.

Soon we were to find that reinforcements were already on their way, although whether they had been alerted by the smoke or someone who had witnessed the attack, I cannot say. ◯

The siege of the Sheriff's House had now lasted six hours. No members of the garrison had been killed but several had been wounded, and all were suffering from fatigue.

As young George Tyrell nursed his wound with one hand and his musket with the other, he began to wonder how much longer they could hold out. As far as they could ascertain, as many as four hundred rebels had fought their way into the garden and some of them had secured a good firing position on a rise covered by fir-trees. Their sporadic firing suggested that they were sparing their ammunition, but it had now become obvious that what they lacked in fire-power, they made up for in determination.

George was thus engrossed in his thoughts when a cry went up from other members of the garrison that reinforcements had arrived. Running to another window, he was delighted to see a contingent of blue-coated cavalry and red-coated foot-soldiers approaching the bridge from the direction of Kinnegad. At the same time, he was amazed to see his father riding out from the house to meet them.

At first George thought his father had taken leave of his senses. Then he realised that there was a lull in the firing. The rebels, it seemed, had been as surprised as they were to see the reinforcements. Taking advantage of the lull, his father succeeded in linking up with the new arrivals and, before the rebels knew what was happening, the cavalry had followed him in through the gates, dragging two pieces of artillery behind them.

As the cavalry scrambled to get their guns into position, the garrison gave them covering fire. It was a volley that was fired with vigour, and George knew that the garrison had been strengthened not only with reinforcements but with hope. A short time later, with the newcomers giving him cover, George's father sallied forth once again, this time with a group of his own men and, after a heated exchanged of gun-fire, drove the rebels from the fir-trees. Seeing them go, George heaved a sigh of relief. At long last, he knew, the siege was over.

O The arrival of reinforcements, wrote Tom Howlett, came as a great blow to the rebel forces. The flying artillery, Colonel Holt called them, for they brought with them two of the heavy guns which he himself considered necessary for victory. Their first round of grapeshot, he told me, killed eight out of fifteen men he had placed in a shrubbery beneath a wall. Several hundred musketmen had then held their ground with great courage and determination, but the artillery fire had continued with murderous effect and they were forced to retreat.

Of these things I knew nothing at the time. I was still lingering near the cottage with my elderly minder, hoping to get a glimpse of Mrs Tyrell as I had never seen the wife of a High Sheriff before. I didn't even realise that a retreat was in progress, until one of the officers went into the cottage and told Mrs Tyrell that she must go with them.

Mrs Tyrell, it seemed, was as high-spirited as her horses. The word spread that she was refusing to go, even when told she could travel in her carriage. It was an interesting situation, and those gathered around the door were curious to see how it was going to be resolved. For the truth was, most of them were accustomed to taking orders from the people in the big houses, not telling them what to do. Then we heard that the officer was insisting that Mrs Tyrell should go with them, as they were taking her as a hostage. O

12

A Battle of Wills

Six o'clock had come and gone. The battle had lasted for almost seven hours and those who had defended the Sheriff's House could hardly believe that they were still alive. As the gunsmoke cleared, George could see that the rebels had melted into the countryside, taking their wounded with them. Many of them had been killed in the battle and their broken bodies lay sprawled in various parts of the courtyard and the gardens, including the burned-out turret from which he and his friends had made their escape.

It was only now they learned that a member of the garrison, who had been shut out when the gates had been closed against the rebels, had succeeded in making the five-mile journey to Kinnegad and raising the alarm. How he had managed to negotiate his way through the rebel lines was a story that George was looking forward to hearing. But first there were other matters to be attended to.

While the reinforcements took over positions on the walls and at the upstairs windows, George's father took stock of the situation. No members of the garrison had been killed, but eight of them had been wounded, several seriously, including Richard Allen. George was saddened to learn that a musket-ball had passed through his cousin's arm and lodged in his side.

George's own wound was only superficial and, when everything had been done to make the more seriously injured as comfortable as possible, he and his brothers went out with their father to survey the battle scene. In the smouldering ruins of the turret in the garden, many bodies were lying on top of one another. As far as they could make out, about twenty-seven rebels had been killed in that particular battle. Others lay among the trees on the rise where they had made their last stand.

Outside the gates, George's father led them past the smouldering ruins of the toll-house and, near the bridge, they stopped at the remains of the cabins which the rebels had also set on fire. More bodies were strewn around the bridge and, in all, they estimated that at least a hundred and fifty of the rebels must have been killed in the siege, not to mention the wounded.

On the way back, Lieutenant Tyrell picked up a long green pennant that had been carried by one of the rebel contingents. George held out the tip of it to reveal that it was decorated with a gold harp and shamrocks.

'God Save Ireland,' said Thomas, reading the words above the harp.

George straightened out the pennant a little more.

'Whitechurch,' read Adam. 'I wonder where that is?'

His father shook his head and, rolling up the pennant, took it into the house. There they found that the condition of Richard Allen, and another of the yeomen, had deteriorated and fears were now being expressed that they might not live. Otherwise, George's father was able to announce, with obvious satisfaction, everyone was present and correct.

It was only then that someone asked about Mrs Tyrell. The question came like a clap of thunder for, in the heat of the battle, they had forgotten all about her. Now they wondered if she had made her way safely to Kilreany, and, if not, what had happened to her. Rushing out of the house, Lieutenant Tyrell called on his sons to come along with him and, catching his horse by the reins, swung into the saddle. George and his brother were about to mount up too, when there was a call from the sentries at the gates informing them that a lady was approaching.

A moment later, to the amazement of all concerned, including the soldiers who had been posted at the top windows, Mrs Tyrell walked in through the gates. She was holding her parasol in one hand, her hat on her head with the other and, as her family ran to meet her, she strolled towards them as serenely as if she had been out for an afternoon walk.

Having noted the carnage that had occurred in the vicinity of the house, Mrs Tyrell made her way through the rubble and into the hall. A quick peep at George's wound assured her that it was nothing serious, although she knew he would probably play it up a bit to impress his brothers. She asserted that she herself was perfectly all right, and soon it became clear that she wasn't going to answer any questions until she had established how everyone else was. She went straight away to the room where Richard and the other wounded members of the garrison lay. On seeing their injuries, she was greatly concerned and was assured that a doctor had been sent for. Nevertheless, she ordered water to be boiled and fresh bandages to be made so that the wounds could be cleansed and, where possible, bound. This she did herself with the help of a soldier who seemed to have had some experience as a medical orderly.

When the doctor finally arrived, the family withdrew so that he might have the space to give the wounded whatever treatment he could offer them. It was only then, when asked once more to tell them what had happened to her, that Mrs Tyrell related how she had been held as a hostage by the rebels.

'But why should they wish to take you hostage?' asked George.

'Well, they didn't make it clear at first that they *were* taking me as a hostage. One of their officers merely told me that I must get into my carriage and go with them.'

'And did you?' asked Thomas. 'Did you get into the carriage?'

'Of course not. Another officer came to see me and was introduced as General Perry – a general, if you don't mind. However, I must admit, he was a man of some sophistication. I told him he could have my carriage and my horses but that he must permit me to remain behind. He was reluctant at first, but eventually agreed. However, after he left, one of the other rebels seized me by the arm and dragged me to the door.'

'The cad,' said Lieutenant Tyrell.

'What happened then?' Adam asked her.

'This fellow – he was a very common sort – told me I must go with them on horseback as the carriage would be needed for some of their wounded. I again appealed to the officers, but I was told I must go with them and remain as a hostage.'

'But why?' George asked her.

'They seemed to be under the impression that one of their officers had been taken prisoner during the battle and I was, I suppose, to be held in exchange for him.'

Lieutenant Tyrell shook his head, as if to say he knew nothing about a prisoner, and she continued, 'Anyway, I was put into the carriage and we had only gone about a mile when this other fellow got into it. He claimed that he had a right to do so, if you don't mind, as he had first obtained it.'

'So he was one of the rebels who first stopped you,' said Adam.

'He may well have been, I can't be sure. In any event, he refused to move, not even for General Perry. Then Mogue Kearns arrived – remember him, we had him as our guest when he was a priest in this area. I implored him to release me, but he just said, "Oh yes, madam," and rode off.'

'So *he* was part of this conspiracy?' said Lieutenant Tyrell. 'The ungrateful lout. To think that we entertained him on several occasions.'

Mrs Tyrell nodded and sighed. 'Yes indeed. Fortunately, another officer came along and told me I was free to go. I think he said his name was Garret Byrne from Ballymanus. However, they kept the horses and the carriage and I had to return by foot. Pity about Veritas. She was the best horse I had.'

'Well, at least you're alive,' said George.

Just then the doctor came into the room and informed them that Richard Allen and one of the yeomen had died of their wounds.

Later that evening, George and his family returned to their own house at Kilreany, only to find that it had been plundered by the rebels.

Tom Howlett had watched the battle of wills between Mrs Tyrell and the rebels with great interest and, in truth, was glad when he saw her being released. It appeared to him that enough lives had already been lost at Clonard and that there was nothing to be gained by the loss of another, especially that of a woman who had taken no part in the hostilities.

After Mrs Tyrell had vacated the carriage, Tom saw some of the more seriously wounded being put on board. All the carts that had been brought along to carry bits and pieces of baggage were also used to transport wounded, and he himself helped by inviting one of the wounded to ride behind him. While most of the rebels had lived to fight another day, he could see the disappointment of defeat etched on their smoke-blackened faces. Hunger and fatigue, he knew, were also gnawing at their souls, and it was a sorry procession that now turned its back on the Sheriff's House and made its way back into the countryside.

From inquiries he made along the way, Tom learned that they were heading for Carbury Castle, about six or seven miles south of Clonard. Soon the stark outline of the castle appeared above the hedgerows; a majestic ruin that rose from the top of a steep hill, its chimneys so tall they seemed to touch the sky.

It was decided that they would spend the night in the safety of the high ground around the castle and, as

darkness eased down on them, Tom wandered through
the camp in search of Colonel Holt and Antrim John.
Many of the rebels were dressing the wounds of their
injured comrades, while others were coming and going on
horseback as they foraged for food in the surrounding
countryside.

When, eventually, Tom made his way up to the castle,
he heard voices raised in anger; the leaders were having a
council of war inside. Sentries who had been posted at
the entrances to ensure that the meeting wasn't disturbed
barred his way, but when he told them he was Colonel
Holt's *aide-de-camp*, he was recognised and allowed in.
The leaders were sitting around a camp-fire amid the
humps and hollows of rubble that littered the floor.
Around the walls, elder bushes and scrub ash had taken
over the castle from its illustrious owners and beneath the
bushes sat a number of other shadowy figures, trusted
aides who listened but did not contribute to the discussion.

Tom was looking for a place to seat himself, when one
of the shadowy figures reached up and pulled him down
beside him. 'Tom boy,' the figure whispered reassuringly,
'it's me – Antrim John.' Turning his head to try and see
the freckled features of his friend in the dark, Tom felt a
great feeling of relief and happiness surge through his
body. He hadn't seen or heard of Antrim John since
before the battle of Clonard and, until that moment,
hadn't known if he was alive or dead. Now they were
back together again and, for the first time in a long while,
a feeling of security returned to him.

Tom was about to say something, but his eyes had
become accustomed to the shadows now and he saw
Antrim John putting a finger to his lips to indicate that he
should remain silent. All eyes and ears were now firmly
focused on what was being said by those gathered around
the camp-fire. Unlike the meeting that had taken place at
Whelp Rock, this had turned into a violent discussion of

what had gone wrong at the Sheriff's House.

Amid claims and counter-claims, Colonel Holt was saying that if they had taken his advice, they could have got two pieces of artillery in Wicklow and done the same damage to the Crown forces that the cavalry had done to them at Clonard.

Father Kearns, on the other hand, was arguing that all the guns and ammunition they needed were in Clonard and that, if they had persisted, they could have had them.

Colonel Holt countered that they could have had a victory – had they sufficient ammunition in the first place. Perhaps, he conceded, if they had persisted they could have had a victory, but, he argued, the cost in terms of human life would have been too great.

As the argument raged, some officers said they couldn't ask their men to continue on the expedition with empty muskets. To this a few hotheads retorted that if they wished to leave they could do so. Counselling patience, others argued that if they kept going they might still succeed in rallying more counties to their cause. However, a few of those who had expressed reluctance to continue could not be persuaded to do otherwise and left the meeting to take their men back home. Colonel Holt, Tom could see, was more convinced now than ever that the odds were stacked against them but agreed to stay.

During the night, Tom heard singing coming from various parts of the camp and couldn't help wondering what on earth the rebels had to sing about. By the time he woke next morning, the wounded had been moved out. Some of the more seriously injured, Antrim John explained, had been taken to the houses of local people who had agreed to hide them. The others had been given enough food to last them for several days and, with the help of companions, would hide out in the woods until they were well enough to try and make their way home.

As the half-light of dawn turned into another sunny day, Tom looked out from the heights of Carbury Castle and surveyed the surrounding countryside. 'Antrim John,' he said. 'Look. You can see the four corners of Ireland from here.'

'Aye, it's a fine view all right,' said his big friend. 'And that,' he added with a smile, 'must surely be Antrim up there to the right.'

'Do you think we'll be able to rally much support?' asked Tom. 'We don't seem to have done very well so far.'

Antrim John shrugged. 'Sure, you never know. And with a bit of luck we might even link up with our friends in the north.'

Away below them Tom watched the rebel army making its way wearily northwards and, somehow in his heart, he knew it had met all the men from the north it was going to meet.

13

The Hooded Horsemen

The sun was high in the sky; it was hot, and Tom unsaddled Betsy so that she could cool down. With a handful of grass, he rubbed her down as best he could and seated himself in the shade of a tree to await the return of Antrim John. Once again he was on a hill and all around him members of the rebel army were resting. Along the way they had seized what provisions they could lay their hands on, but now mutton was on the menu as foraging parties had brought back sheep.

Antrim John had been with one of the foraging parties and, when he joined Tom, he informed him that most of horsemen had gone out again. 'There are a lot of mouths to feed,' he said. 'We'll need all the sheep we can find.'

'How many do you think there are?' Tom asked his friend.

'You mean sheep?'

Tom shook his head. 'No, I mean, how many men are there left?'

Antrim John shrugged. 'Hard to say. We probably lost about sixty at Clonard. Then we've left behind the wounded and the faint-hearted. I'd say we've still got three to four thousand.'

'I see some of them are drinking.'

Antrim John nodded. 'I know. I suppose it's hard to blame them. They must be sick and tired of it all by this stage.'

'Where did they get it?'

'When we were camped at Carbury Castle, one of the foraging parties came across a big house. Somebody said it was Newberry Hall, home of Lord Harberton, whoever he is. Anyway, they raided his wine-cellar. We had some of it last night. It was good too.'

Tom grunted. 'I wondered what all the singing was about.'

Everyone, it seemed, was waiting for the mutton to boil. Antrim John opened his tunic and, lying back full-length in the grass, put his hat over his face. Soon, it became obvious that he was dozing, so Tom leaned back against the trunk of the tree and took his journal out of his school-bag. During the stop-over at Carbury Castle, he had managed to jot down an account of some of the things he had seen at Clonard. But so much had happened. There were so many things to record. And then there was the disagreement he had witnessed at the castle.

Letting his head loll back, Tom closed his eyes and was wondering what to write down next when he heard a commotion in the camp. Scrambling to his feet, he saw that Antrim John was already on his way down to find out what the matter was. Running after him, he found Colonel Holt remonstrating with some of his men who were drinking and in an obvious state of intoxication. In addition to the wine, it appeared that two small barrels of whiskey had been taken from Lord Harberton's cellar and many of the men had been helping themselves to the contents.

Incensed, Colonel Holt rushed over, smashed in the end of the barrels with the butt of a musket, and turned them upside down to pour the whiskey out. Many of those who had been drinking immediately rose to their feet and, fortified by the whiskey they had already consumed, threatened to kill him. Undeterred, Colonel Holt pointed out that it was they who would be killed if they didn't stop drinking, for if they were attacked they wouldn't be able to defend themselves.

This, Tom reckoned, was sound advice and it seemed to have a sobering effect on those involved. No sooner had they sat down again, however, than there was a warning shot from the look-outs. Colonel Holt immediately called his men to arms, only to find that as few as two hundred of them were in a fit state to fight. Several hundred others who seemed to be lying on the ground resting were, in fact, in a state of intoxication. Rushing in among them, he endeavoured to rouse as many as possible.

'Come on,' said Antrim John and, catching Tom by the arm, ran with him back to the horses.

Tom lifted his saddle, but his friend shouted, 'Leave it. There's no time.'

Antrim John was already on his own horse and, swinging up on to Betsy's bare back, Tom galloped after him.

Colonel Holt, Tom could see, was still trying to rally his men, but without much success. Stupefied with drink and fatigue, many of them were struggling to their feet, unaware of the danger they were in. Others who had not been drinking, looked on in dismay. Their horsemen were still out foraging for food, they themselves had little ammunition left, and now many of their comrades were in a state of intoxication. Hearing a volley of shots from the cornfields at the bottom of the hill, many of them broke ranks and scattered in confusion.

Sticking as close to Antrim John as he could, Tom could see a large contingent of blue-coated cavalrymen moving in through the cornfields. There were, he reckoned, at least two hundred of them, and they were followed by a long line of red-coated foot-soldiers. The volley of shots had failed to stop the advance, and now the cavalry were slashing at the musketmen with their sabres. The musketmen appeared to be out of ammunition and were falling before the sabres like stalks of corn before a reaping-hook. The foot-soldiers who followed had fixed their long-bladed bayonets to the end of their muskets and were making sure that none survived.

Colonel Holt was now trying to rally as many of his

'I saw a pale horse ... I knew his name was Death'

men as possible to try and cover the retreat. Those with ammunition, and in a fit condition to do so, were ordered to keep up a steady fire on their pursuers, while others were told to burn the houses along the roadside so as to create a smoke-screen. The horsemen who had been foraging had now returned, and were riding in and out of the smoke as they tried to keep the cavalry at bay.

It was only when Betsy's forelegs began to sink, and she pulled away to one side in an effort to extricate herself, that Tom realised they had been driven into a bog. A few more violent plunges and he felt as if he was on a bucking bronco. Without a saddle to hold on to, he found himself sailing through the air. His head hit a piece of bog-oak and the battle faded from his consciousness.

O I was in that other world, Tom was to recall, where I could see many things and yet was not a part of them. It was not the world of man and swords, of sun and corn, but of darkness, where everything was within my very being yet separate from it. Yet, it was a darkness in which I could see and, when a shadow moved above me, I beheld a great bird, like a vulture, only it had six wings and was full of eyes. And almost as if I was flying with it, I saw it land beside three other beasts. One was like a lion, one like a calf, the third like a man. However, each, like the bird, had six wings and was full of eyes. In the middle of them stood a lamb that had been slain, and the lamb had seven horns and seven eyes.

Once again I knew I was seeing those things that my father had so often read to me from the Book of Revelations, for I heard the great bird saying, 'Come and see.' And when I looked, I saw a pale horse. The rider wore a black hood and a long black cloak and, while I could not see his face, I knew his name was Death. 'And hell followed with him,' a voice was saying. 'And power was given unto them over the fourth part of the earth, to kill with sword and with hunger...'

Now I could see the pale horse moving about the bog and its hooded rider looking at the corpses of those who had been killed in their flight from the cavalry. And in his right hand he held up a sword, on the end of which was a skull, and I knew he was parading it through the dead in the same way that Hunter Gowan and the Black Mob had paraded the rebel's finger through the town of Gorey.

It was then that I became aware of another hooded figure, the figure of a woman. The pale horse and its rider had gone, and the hooded figure was alone on the field of death. Gliding among the fallen, she stooped occasionally to pick things up and put them under her long dark cloak. I tried to cry out, to protest that she was robbing the dead, but as she stooped she turned and smiled. It was a hideous smile and suddenly I realised that she was the Moving Magazine. But if she heard my cry for help, she paid no further heed to it. I tried to get up, to follow her, but I was held to the ground as if by some invisible power. I could not move, nor could I stop the hooded woman from leaving me and soon I was left alone again.

All this time, nothing else stirred on the landscape. No breeze to stir the leaves and make them rustle, no joy to stir the birds to song, no breath to stir the dead to life. And then, standing a short distance away, I saw a young woman. Her long red hair and flowing dress were in colourful contrast to the world of darkness around her, and she was smiling. She also had the tip of her forefinger in her mouth, and she lowered her head in a way that seemed to tease, almost as if she was inviting me to come and join her. Then my heart raced, for I could see it was Croppy Biddy. Again, I stretched my hand towards her and tried to rise, but she just turned and, with a skip in her step, disappeared into the darkness that was the emptiness of my soul.

For what seemed an eternity, I had seen much but heard little from those who had flitted in and out of my mind, and then, as if from afar, I heard the words, 'Tom boy.

Tom boy.' Or was it just the throbbing of my head that I heard? No, there it was again. 'Tom boy. Tom boy. Wake up. Slowly I opened my eyes and, seeing a mop of red hair slowly come into focus, I whispered, 'Croppy Biddy?'

'It's me, Tom,' said the figure that crouched over me. 'It's me. Antrim John.'

Afraid that I might reach out once more and find nothing there, I slowly raised my hand. 'Antrim John,' I asked. 'Is it really you?'

The freckled face above me nodded, saying, 'Aye, Tom, it's really me.' At the same time, my hand touched his face. Overjoyed, I could only lie back and sob, for I had seen a pale horse and Death was its rider, and I knew I had come back from the brink of Hell. ○

Seeing Tom reach out for his school-bag, Antrim John told him, 'Better hide your journal. If you're found with that they'll hang you.' At the same time he picked up Tom's pistols, which were lying on the ground and, stuffing them in under a turf bank, added, 'These too.'

Tom struggled to his feet and, taking the journal from the bag, tucked it in under his shirt. 'Betsy,' he exclaimed, suddenly remembering that he had taken a fall. 'Have you seen Betsy anywhere?'

'Betsy's fine. She's over there.'

To his great delight, Tom saw Betsy standing on a piece of firm ground not far distant, her reins hanging loosely from her bridle. 'Once we got into the bog,' he explained, 'I couldn't hold on, not without a saddle. I think I hit my head on something.'

'It's just as well,' said Antrim John. 'The cavalry must have left you for dead.'

'What about Colonel Joe?'

Antrim John shook his head. 'Many of our men were killed here in the bog. The others were dispersed. I can't find him anywhere.'

Picking up Betsy's reins, Tom led her out of the bog

and on to firmer ground. The bog was littered with the bodies of rebels. 'And how did you escape?'

Antrim John shrugged. 'The main part of our forces escaped, thanks to Colonel Joe's rearguard action. If he hadn't set up a smoke-screen and engaged the cavalry, they might all have been killed.'

'Where are they now?'

'I don't know. I fought with them until we managed to disengage. Then I made my way back to see if I could find anyone alive.'

'I'm glad you did,' said Tom. 'But I wonder what's happened to Colonel Joe?'

Antrim John shook his head. 'I wish I knew. But don't you worry. He can take care of himself.'

Many horses had also been killed in the battle and taking a saddle from one of them, Antrim John strapped it on to Betsy. 'Now Tom boy,' he said, giving him a leg up. 'You take it easy. Next house we come to, we'll get that head of yours seen to.'

Not far from the bog they came across several cabins but found that the doors were closed. The occupants, they reckoned, had either fled or were too scared to open up to strangers. They kept going and, towards evening, had put a good distance between themselves and the scene of the battle. They had almost given up hope of receiving any hospitality when, to their great relief, one door was opened and they were welcomed inside. Soon they were seated at the open fire and, as the woman of the house tended to Tom's injured head, she told them that she had been greatly distressed by all the killing that had taken place. In particular, she said, she was sorry to hear of the death of Colonel Holt.

Startled, Tom turned his head and asked her, 'How do you know he's dead?'

Realising that she had given him a shock, the woman glanced across at Antrim John. 'But, alanna, sure, everyone knows it. Wasn't he shot crossing Longwood Bog.'

14

A Gift of Silver

It was with a heavy heart that Tom Howlett resumed his journey next morning. The great adventure on which he had embarked with such excitement and anticipation had come crashing down around him. The great army of men he had watched streaming down from Whelp Rock on their expedition northwards, had been dispersed. The dead lay rotting on Longwood Bog, their flags trampled into the pools of peaty water by the hooves of the horses that had over-run them. The injured had crawled away to hide, and in many cases to die. As for the survivors, many of them, according to Antrim John, would now be hunted down and killed.

'But you said the main part of our forces had escaped,' said Tom. 'Thanks to Colonel Joe.'

Antrim John, who was walking ahead, leading Betsy, replied, 'So they did, Tom boy, so they did. From what that woman told me last night, it appears that about fifteen hundred of them have continued on northwards. The rest have split up, and will probably try and make their way back home. But don't think for a moment the cavalry are going to leave it at that. They'll follow them, harass them at every opportunity. They have them on the run now, and they know it.'

'And what about us?' asked Tom. 'Do you think they'll come after us too?'

Antrim John kept walking. 'They seem to have gone after the main body and left us behind. If we can find the road down into Dublin we should be all right. They won't be expecting any of us to be seen on that.'

Tom twisted himself around in the saddle to glance back and, seeing that they weren't being followed, said, 'Do you think Colonel Joe is really dead?'

Antrim John shook his head. 'I don't know.'

'But surely you would have found him if he was.'

'Well, I looked hard enough, but there were a lot of dead. I could have missed him.'

As the sun rose it became hotter. Tom dismounted so as to give Betsy a rest and walked on, side by side, with his big Antrim friend. A short time later they felt the need for a rest themselves and sat down in the shade of a hazel-covered hill. The woman who had extended them the hospitality of her home had also given them some food to eat along the way. This they shared and were lying face down to have a drink of spring water when, to their surprise, they heard laughter coming from the hill.

'Sounds like a woman,' whispered Tom.

'Wait here,' said Antrim John and, crouching as he ran, he disappeared in under the bushes.

A few moments later Tom heard his friend calling on him and, when he joined him, found to his surprise that several other survivors of the battle had stopped beneath the hazels for a rest. One of them was an old woman who appeared to have been drinking.

'She says her name is Katty Kearns,' said one of the men. 'From Wicklow.'

'And what's she doing here?' asked Antrim John.

'Sir,' said the woman, speaking up for herself, 'I came with my husband for fear of the soldiers.'

'Well, you'd better keep quiet,' Antrim John warned her, 'or the soldiers will find you and we'll all be in trouble.' Catching the smell of whiskey from her breath, he asked, 'And tell me, Missus, where did you get the drink?'

'A United Irishman gave it to us,' the woman replied, 'He was in the Corps of Cavalry.'

'Ah, hush woman,' said one of the men. 'You're talking nonsense.'

'It's the drink talking,' laughed another.

'I beg your pardon,' protested the old woman, 'it is not

the drink talking. I just had one glass of whiskey. If you don't believe me, ask Colonel Holt.'

'Colonel Joe!' exclaimed Tom. 'But we were told he was dead.'

'They said he was shot crossing Longwood Bog,' added Antrim John.

The old woman threw back her head and cackled with laughter again. 'Dead? He's not dead. Or if he is I've been drinking with his ghost!'

'Mrs Kearns,' said Antrim John sternly. 'Be serious. Did you really see Colonel Holt?'

'I *am* serious,' protested the old woman. 'I was in this cabin, on the edge of the bog. The man let me in, you see. That's why I wasn't killed by the soldiers. And who should come in, but Colonel Holt. He was wounded. Then another man gave us directions, and someone else gave us food. A nice fowl, a plate of potatoes and a bottle of whiskey.' She laughed again, saying, 'I can't remember where we went after that. But he's gone now.'

'Mrs Kearns,' said Tom, 'was he badly injured?'

'No worse than yourself, son,' she told him. 'Nothing a drop of whiskey couldn't cure.' With that she gave another cackle of laughter and, taking a whiskey bottle out from beneath her clothes, drained a sip that had been left in the bottom.

'Come on, Tom boy,' said Antrim John, rising to his feet. 'Time we were on our way. Maybe we can catch up with him.'

'Can we come with you?' asked one of the others.

Antrim John shook his head. 'Too dangerous. Better split up.'

'And what about her?' asked another.

Antrim John smiled. 'I don't think she's in any danger. When she sobers up, she can make her own way home.'

Antrim John gave Tom a leg up and, as they continued their journey, they discussed some of the things the old woman had said.

'Do you really think Colonel Joe may still be alive?' asked Tom.

'Aye,' replied Antrim John, 'I think he might.'

'You don't think it was just the drink talking?'

'Well, the drink can make you forget, but, then again, it can also loosen your tongue. And she's from Wicklow herself, remember, so she probably knows him.'

'So, where are we heading now?'

'A safe house.' Antrim John smiled. 'While you were resting that sore head of yours, the woman in the cabin gave me directions.'

Tom couldn't help feeling guilty that they hadn't told the people they had met in the hazels that they were heading for a safe house, but Antrim John told him not to be silly. 'It's every man for himself now,' he said, 'and if we told everybody we met where we were going, it wouldn't be a safe house for very long.'

'That woman, the one back in the cabin who told you how to get to it,' said Tom. 'She didn't tell us her name.'

'That's right. Nor did she say who to ask for when we get there.'

'Why not?'

Antrim John stopped and, turning around, explained, 'Because we don't want to know.' Seeing that his young friend didn't understand, he added, 'Listen, Tom boy. If we don't know their names, we can't tell anybody, right?'

'You mean, if we're caught?'

Antrim John nodded. 'Precisely.'

The directions they had been given were good and soon they came to a large farmhouse. The door was opened by a young woman and Tom watched as Antrim John spoke quietly to her and shook her hand. One way or other, he suspected, a signal was passed, for the woman invited them in.

○ My nostrils, Tom later wrote, were immediately assailed by an aroma which reminded me of my home in the Avoca valley. It was a wholesome smell, a smell of churned milk and baking, and it took my mind back to the days when I waited with great anticipation for the warm cakes of oaten bread to come off the griddle. Only now did I realise how long it had been since I had eaten freshly baked food.

There was an old man sitting by the open fire. He had a well-smoked clay pipe in his right hand and he motioned with it, indicating to us that we should pull up a stool and sit down. He said little if anything thereafter, but we knew from his general demeanour that we were welcome at his hearth. No sooner had we sat down than the young woman was joined by an older woman and together they tended to our every need. Seeing how much we savoured the aroma of their baking, they immediately gave us cakes of oaten bread and buttermilk. They brought us clean clothes and took our old ones for washing, and they brought us hot water to bathe our feet. So comforting was this that I only remembered about the injury to my head when the older woman began to clean it. She asked me where I was from and what had befallen me and, when I told her, she related how she had recently treated someone else from Wicklow who had suffered a similar injury.

Hardly daring to hope, I looked up at her and asked her who it was. 'I was telling him,' she replied, 'how sorry I was to hear of the death of Colonel Holt, when he turned and said, "My good woman, I am Holt." '

It was then we knew that even though she had been drinking, old Katty Kearns had been speaking the truth when she had told us that Colonel Joe was alive. ○

As the older woman tended to Tom's head, she continued to talk and bit by bit they learned what had happened to Colonel Holt.

'He had a wound on his head and left arm,' she went on. 'He said he was crossing a ditch when the top of it gave way, bringing both himself and his horse to the ground. The soldiers were shooting as fast as they could load and fire. Men were falling all around him, his head was bleeding and he only survived by pretending to be dead.'

'That was a smart move,' said Antrim John. 'If he had been caught he would have been executed.'

'Anyway,' the woman continued, 'he told me that when the soldiers had passed he came across a number of women who were crying. He said they were upset at all the killing, for the soldiers spared no one. Then a woman took pity on him, even though she was the wife of a yeoman, and washed his coat and gave him food.'

By this stage the older woman was wrapping a bandage around Tom's head, and he heard the younger woman saying, 'In return for her kindness he gave the yeoman's wife his silver-mounted sword and his silver-mounted bridle, and he told her to go to where his horse had fallen and that she would find a pair of silver-mounted pistols.'

Turning his head slightly, Tom could see that Antrim John was smiling and he knew his big friend was thinking the same as he was. Any doubts they might have had were gone. Colonel Holt, they now knew for certain, had survived the battle and, like themselves, was making his way back to Wicklow.

'At one stage,' the younger woman continued, 'he was almost caught by a patrol. But instead of running he marched up to them, as bold as you like, and asked them which way the rebels had gone?'

Antrim John shook his head as if to say that that was asking for trouble. 'And how did they react?'

The younger woman smiled. 'They asked him what he wanted to know for? So he just showed them the wound on his head. He said he had almost been scalped by a musket-ball and that the rebels had robbed him of his horse.'

Antrim John shook his head again, saying, 'Oh, that's him all right.'

'They let him pass,' the younger woman went on, 'but then he almost came to grief when he met some old woman. I think he said her name was Kearns.'

'That's right,' said Tom. 'Katty Kearns. We met her back there a bit. She said she had been drinking with him.'

The younger woman smiled. 'Well, from what I gather, he accompanied her part of the way. But during their travels someone gave them a bottle of whiskey and she became a bit boisterous, so he had to continue without her.'

'At first,' said the older woman, taking up the story again, 'he steered a course by observing the sun. But then several of our friends helped him and one of them gave him directions to come here.'

Antrim John was drying his feet now, having enjoyed giving them such a good soak in the warm water. 'Where do you think he might be now?' he asked.

The younger woman shook her head. 'He said he was heading for Dublin, but where he might find another safe house, I couldn't say.'

The older woman, who had been coming and going with hot water and other bits and pieces, stopped when she heard this and whispered, 'He told me he was heading for the Enchanted House, wherever that is. He said he would be safe when he reached it.'

During the afternoon, Tom and Antrim John dried their clothes at the open fire and, when evening came, were invited to sit down at a large table in another room for something to eat. It was only then, when several figures emerged from the shadows to join them, that they realised there were other rebels in the house. These, they learned, had arrived before them and had been sleeping somewhere out at the back. All were bandaged in one way or another. They were thin, almost frail, Tom thought, and were rather pathetic-looking creatures.

The two women of the house hadn't stopped working all day and now they arrived from the kitchen with a dozen or more large cakes of hot oaten bread. Having satisfied their hunger, the other rebels then demonstrated a great hunger for information about what exactly had happened during the battle. Soon they were vying with one another to tell what they knew, especially how they themselves had escaped either the muskets of the foot-soldiers or the sabres of the cavalry. For the first time now, Tom learned that all the other rebel leaders had escaped with the bulk of their forces, and none of those gathered around the table was in any doubt that this was due to the smoke-screen set up by Colonel Holt.

Weary of all the talk of war, Tom eventually excused himself and made his way upstairs to a small back room where the women had kindly told him he could spend the night. It was a long time since he had slept in a proper bed and, as he snuggled in, he couldn't help wishing he was back in his own house in the Avoca valley. Perhaps it was the smell he had got in the kitchen that made him lonely, the smell of home cooking. He didn't know but, for whatever reason, he began to cry, and he was glad that Antrim John couldn't hear him.

Morning came, the tears of darkness had gone, a blue sky promised another sunny day, and it was time to be going. Having thanked the people of the house for all their kindness, Tom and Antrim John took their leave. Betsy was well rested now too and, having mounted up, Tom followed his big friend across the fields. Soon they were on the Dublin road and were congratulating themselves on their good fortune when, without warning, they found their way barred by a group of soldiers on horseback, their sabres drawn, ready for action. To his dismay, Tom noted that the blades of the sabres were dull and did not glint in the morning sun. They were still matted and stained with the blood of battle.

15

Walking on Eggshells

O Never before, Tom confided in his journal, did I feel so close to death, not even on the day I was chased by Hunter Gowan and the Black Mob. When we found our way barred by the soldiers, I trembled with fear. I had often heard that animals could smell a person's fear, and I have no doubt that Betsy sensed my fear on that awful occasion. Normally a most placid animal, she raised her head and flared her nostrils. Her big eyes were rolling in her head and I knew she was as terrified as I was.

The soldiers were wearing furry helmets and blue tunics and at first I thought they were yeomen. That fact alone was enough to strike fear in my heart, for I had often heard how ruthless yeoman could be. According to my father, they were recruited from the local loyalist population by people who lived in the big houses. For this reason, they knew the locality and the local people well and they never hesitated to execute those they suspected of disloyalty, whether by hanging them on the spot or by a slash of a sabre. Imagine my feelings then as I looked upon their sabres, knowing that my blood and that of Antrim John might be dripping from them at any moment.

When the officer in charge of the soldiers spoke, however, I knew by his accent that they were not yeomen but British cavalrymen, During our travels I had heard the rebels call them light dragoons and I was aware that they were capable of great cruelty too. At the same time it occurred to me that we might be able to talk our way out of the situation. Being from Britain they might not know the locality as well as the yeomen, or be able to place our accents with the same degree of accuracy.

Fortunately, the women who had shown us such gracious hospitality at the farmhouse had also suggested that we should have a story ready for just such an eventuality. As a result Antrim John was quick to respond when the officer, a young man, asked us where we had come from.

'We're from Newberry Hall,' he told them. 'It's been sacked by the rebels. We were lucky to escape with our lives.'

'But Newberry Hall is to the south of here,' said the officer, displaying a little more knowledge than we had hoped for.

'To be sure it is,' replied Antrim John, putting on a bit of a southern accent. 'But after we got away we decided to head for the Dublin road. We knew the rebels wouldn't dare use it, and we would have a better chance of finding the safety of the military.'

'What happened to the lad?' asked the officer.

'My son, Tom,' said Antrim John, turning his head to acknowledge me. 'The shaft of a pike. Nearly took the head off him. We were lucky to get away. They've wrecked the place, you know. Cleaned it out entirely, cellar and all.'

'The bag,' said the officer, reaching out his sabre so that I could hang my school-bag on the point of it.

Thanks to the foresight of the young woman at the farmhouse, my books had been removed and replaced with bread for the journey. The officer handed it back to me, and as he did so I prayed that he wouldn't search me and find the journal which I had hidden under my shirt.

'You've a northern accent,' said the officer, turning his attention to Antrim John again.

Now, Antrim John had no more of a Cavan accent than I had, but he replied, 'Cavan. I come from Cavan. Lord Harberton gave me a job when I came looking for work. He was very good to me. He was very good to all the people in the locality, and this is how they repay him.'

'Is Lord Harberton still alive?' asked the officer.

For a moment I thought Antrim John had been caught out, but he just smiled a big freckled smile and said, 'Well, you know yourself, Sir, the title never dies, not as long as there's a son to carry it on. You know the saying, the king is dead, long live the king.'

The reference to a king seemed to please the officer, and he smiled, saying, 'Well put.'

The soldiers had lowered their sabres now, not fully, but enough to indicate that they were less suspicious of us than they were.

'And why are you going to Dublin?' asked the officer.

'The family have a house in Dublin,' said Antrim John. 'They must be told what has happened.'

The officer nodded. 'They probably know by now. Very well, you may proceed. But take care. We routed these scoundrels at Longwood Bog and they're on the run.'

Antrim John thanked the officer for his advice and, with indescribable relief, we saw the wall of sabres opening up before us. Soon we were on our way again and, whatever about Antrim John, I said a fervent prayer of thanks to my Maker for delivering us from what I knew was almost certain death. ○

Shortly after their encounter with the dragoons, Antrim John called a halt. They had come to an inn and, whether it was because of the heat or their close brush with death, Tom didn't know, but his friend informed him that he was powerful thirsty. While the big man went inside to get some ale, Tom unsaddled Betsy whom he found had also developed a substantial thirst. After the mare had filled her belly from a stone trough in the back yard, he rubbed her down with a handful of straw before tending to his own needs. Sitting on the edge of the trough, he couldn't help thinking of what had happened and found himself saying another prayer in thanksgiving for the fact that they were still alive. At the same time he felt his shirt to make sure the journal was still there, then helped himself to some oaten bread.

When Antrim John emerged from the inn, Tom learned that he had discovered some interesting information. The landlord, it appeared, wasn't a United Irishman, but was not unsympathetic to those who were. Someone answering the description of Colonel Holt had, he confided, called there early in the morning. After hiding in the barn, where he had enjoyed two pots of mulled ale, he had hailed a passing cart.

'What sort of cart?' asked Tom, as they resumed their journey.

Antrim John wiped his mouth on his sleeve. 'Well, it appears there were three carts. They were bringing eggs from Castlepollard in County Westmeath.'

'So he probably has a good chance of making it safely to Dublin?'

'Probably. But getting through Dublin city is another matter.' Antrim John was thoughtful for a moment before adding, 'He may be riding on eggs now, but he'll be walking on eggshells when he gets to the city. We all will.'

Tom laughed. 'That's a funny thing to say.'

'There's nothing funny about it,' said Antrim John. 'What I mean is, we'll have to tread very carefully. From what I hear, Dublin is full of Government spies – not to mention the military. Mark my words, they'll be on the look-out for people like us, rebels trying to get back to Wicklow and Wexford. One wrong move, one wrong word, and we'll be in trouble.'

'It looks as if Colonel Joe knows a safe house there,' said Tom. 'Remember what he told the women at the farmhouse?'

Antrim John nodded. 'Aye, he said he would be safe once he reached the Enchanted House. But that's no good to us, unless we can figure out what he meant. What do you think?'

Tom shook his head. 'I don't know.' They lapsed into

silence, each wondering what Colonel Joe could possibly have meant, but by the time they reached the outskirts of Dublin they were none the wiser.

It was late now and, in the half-light of the summer night, the two travellers stopped to look at the dark outline of the city which was etched against a purple sky. Lights twinkled from the windows of houses and taverns and they were bigger and brighter than the stars which were small and pale and distant.

The city, Tom could see, was a big place, and he couldn't help wondering how they were going to find their way through it, let alone find Colonel Holt. As they crossed the River Liffey, the stench of the city's sewage forced them to hurry to the other end of the bridge. Then, almost as if to compensate, a sweeter, tantalising smell caressed their nostrils.

Not knowing which way they should go, Antrim John nipped into an ale-house to inquire. They were half way up a narrow cobble-stoned street and, as he waited, Tom savoured the sweet smell again. Somehow it reminded him of home cooking and he wondered once again what it was.

When Antrim John came out he announced that he had been directed to go to an inn called the Brazen Head. 'It's a meeting place for the United Irishmen,' he whispered.

'How do you know?' asked Tom.

'A man I met inside. I gave him a signal and he responded. He was one of ours.'

The Brazen Head, they discovered, was only a short distance down the quays and was close to the river. Once again Tom dismounted while his friend made discreet inquiries inside. As he waited, a well-dressed man rode into the yard and disappeared round the back. Above the inn were a number of windows and he reckoned that many a traveller spent the night there before riding on into the city, rested and refreshed for whatever business he had to do.

A short time later, the street was filled with raucous laughter and Tom saw several men arrive on foot. One of them twiddled a silver-handled cane in his hand and all talked out loud in a way that suggested that they wanted not only to be seen but heard. Other, less pretentious figures, kept to the shadows, not wanting to be seen or heard.

Suddenly Tom became aware of another group of men approaching and, pulling Betsy after him, retreated into the shadows himself. He had seen a glint of metal on the men's chests and realised immediately that they were soldiers. Each soldier, he knew, wore a metal badge where the two white helts crossed in front of the red tunic.

Hardly daring to breathe, Tom cupped his hand over the mare's nostrils in an effort to keep her quiet. Betsy, however, was restless. She tossed her head and pawed the cobble-stones and there was nothing he could do to stop her.

'Who goes there?' demanded one of the soldiers.

'It...it...it's just me,' Tom stammered.

'Come into the light so that we can see you,' ordered another.

Gingerly, Tom edged forward until he was framed in the light from the windows of the inn. The soldiers, he could see, had levelled their muskets in his direction. There were sharp-pointed bayonets on the end of them and one of these was now thrust up to his face as the soldiers demanded to know who he was and why he had been hiding.

'I wasn't hiding, I'm... I'm...' From the few words that had been said, Tom realised that the soldiers were Dubliners, probably militiamen. Somehow he felt they wouldn't accept the story about Lord Harberton as readily as the others had. And he didn't think it would sound as plausible coming from him as it had coming from Antrim John. Furthermore, he reckoned, it would be inviting trouble to suggest that he had just come from

Tom faces a bayonet at the Brazen Head

Meath. So, on the spur of the moment, he said, 'I'm holding the horse for a gentleman.'

The soldiers looked at Betsy and one observed, 'That nag?'

'That's not the horse of a gentleman,' said another.

'It is too,' Tom insisted. 'He's gone inside. He said he would reward me well if I looked after her.'

'Did he now?' said one of the soldiers and, pushing Tom towards the doorway of the inn, told him, 'Go on then, show us this gentleman. Maybe he'll reward us too.'

The others laughed and, with a bayonet prodding the small of his back, Tom was marched inside.

The inn was full, but the babble of voices fell silent when the presence of the soldiers was observed.

Speaking loudly, for all to hear, one of the soldiers asked, 'Well? Where is this gentleman of yours? Point him out.'

Tom looked around. He could see Antrim John with a group of men over by another door. Desperately, he wondered what to do. 'I...I... don't see him.'

'But he must be here,' said one of the soldiers. 'Weren't you minding his horse?'

'Maybe he's not looking hard enough,' said another soldier. With that, Tom felt a push in the back and found himself sprawling on the floor. Wondering what to do, he cast a desperate glance behind him. To his surprise he discovered that a number of customers had somehow managed to get in the way, and were now between him and the soldiers. At the same time a man helped him to his feet, saying, 'Follow me.'

There was a lot of shouting and scuffling as the soldiers tried to clear the way and, before Tom knew it, he was ushered out through a side door. Moments later, he found himself at the front of the inn with Antrim John and the man who had come to his aid.

'Who are you?' asked Antrim John.

The stranger looked up and down the street. 'No time

for introductions. Quickly, come this way.'

'I have to get my horse,' Tom panted.

'Not now,' the stranger told him. 'You must get away. We'll get the horse later.'

Taking to their heels, they followed the stranger up the street, which rose steeply from the river and, when he turned in to the right they did likewise, keeping close to him as he ran through a maze of dark alleyways. A short time later they emerged into another street at the top of the hill and paused for breath. There were many taverns in this street, they could see, but the stranger led them straight across and down into another maze of side streets and alleys. Then, almost before they knew what was happening, a door opened, the stranger disappeared, and they found themselves in the darkenened room of a small house. A voice from within told them to be quiet and, with hearts beating wildly, they listened to the pounding of boots on the cobble-stones outside. A group of soldiers had run on past and, weird as it might seem, the words of Antrim John now came to Tom's mind. 'When we get to the city,' he had warned, 'We'll be walking on eggshells. One wrong move, one wrong word, and we'll be in trouble.'

16

Escape from the City

When the danger had passed, candles were lit and Tom could see that they were in the house of a handloom weaver.

'Where are we?' asked Antrim John.

A man, whom they took to be the weaver, brought one of the candles over to the table, while his wife made sure that the small windows at the front were well covered.

'You're in a safe house,' the man told him.

Antrim John nodded. 'Young Tom here, and myself, we're very grateful.'

'No need,' the woman assured him. 'We heard things didn't go well in Meath.'

Antrim John shook his head. 'How did you know?' The woman busied herself at the open fire. 'There were others before you. They told us what happened.'

'They'll be from Wicklow and Wexford,' said Tom.

'Dublin too,' the man informed them.

It was the first time Tom knew that there had been Dubliners in the battle of Clonard.

'What part of Dublin are we in?' asked Antrim John.

'The Liberties,' the man replied.

'There's always been great support for the United Irishmen in this part of the city,' said the woman.

'So it's safe then?' said Antrim John.

'The safest place in the city,' the man told him, 'but the most dangerous.'

'How do you mean?' asked Tom.

'What he means,' said the woman, 'is that we're just beside Dublin Castle. The police have their headquarters in there and they're very active here.'

When Antrim John told them what had happened at the Brazen Head, the man said, 'You're lucky it was the

120

militia that came across you, not the police. If it had been
Major Sirr and his men you'd have been in real trouble.'

The name of Major Sirr was new to both Tom and
Antrim John and, when they asked who he was, they were
told he was the Dublin's notorious chief of police. For his
part, Tom now felt very much a country boy, ignorant of
what was going on in the big city. Then, as they talked, he
learned that their hosts had never heard of Hunter
Gowan and the Black Mob. That made him feel better,
but not for long. As they heard more about the activities
of Major Sirr, he began to feel distinctly uneasy.

'I was told the Brazen Head was a meeting-place for
our people,' said Antrim John.

'So it is,' the man told him, 'or should I say *was*. But a
lot of our people still frequent it. That's why the military
have been keeping an eye on it… not to mention Major
Sirr. It was just opposite the Brazen Head, in Oliver
Bond's house, that Sirr and his men arrested some of our
leaders last March.'

'Is that when they got Lord Edward Fitzgerald?' asked
Antrim John.

The weaver shook his head. 'No. He wasn't arrested
until May, just a few days before the rebellion broke out.
He had been staying in a safe house up in Thomas
Street.'

'You crossed Thomas Street on the way here,' the
woman explained.

'He had been staying at different places,' the man
continued, 'and then he moved into the house of Mr
Murphy, the feather merchant.'

The woman, who was now getting her visitors something to eat, turned from the fire and recalled, 'I
remember it well. The word in the street was that he had
a heavy cold and a sore throat, so he stayed in bed.
During the day someone called with his uniform – a
lovely uniform it was too – a dark green suit with braid, a
crimson cape and the cap of liberty.'

'How do you know?' asked Tom.

'Wasn't it carried back to the castle by the soldiers,' the woman told him. 'They held it up so everybody could see it.'

'They came for him about seven in the evening,' the man continued. 'Mr Murphy had gone up to the bedroom to tell him he had a drink of whey ready for him. Unfortunately, the front door had been left open and, before they knew what was happening, two officers burst into the room. According to Mr Murphy, his lordship sprang up like a tiger and grappled with them. During the struggle, one of them fired a shot at him but missed. He stabbed both of them with his dagger, but then Major Sirr arrived and shot him in the shoulder.'

'Was he killed?' asked Tom.

The weaver shook his head. 'No, but he didn't live very long after that.'

'The soldiers tied him to an open sedan-chair and paraded him up to the castle,' said the woman. 'He died in Newgate prison, over there on the other side of the Liffey, at the beginning of June.'

'And what about Colonel Holt?' asked Tom. 'Have you heard any word of him?'

The man nodded. 'He passed a signal to one of our people as he went through Thomas Street yesterday. We kept an eye on him, but as he was going through Harold's Cross on the way out of the city he was recognised by a woman from Wicklow, who alerted the military.'

Tom jumped to his feet. 'He wasn't captured, was he?'

'No, he's all right,' the man assured him. 'When the cavalry came, he hid behind a wall. They couldn't find anybody who had seen anyone answering his description. So they went off looking for him. When the coast was clear, he headed for the mountains.'

'He said he was heading for the Enchanted House,' said Antrim John. 'Wherever that is.'

'He seemed to think he would be safe when he reached

it,' Tom added. 'Have you any idea where it might be?'

The weaver looked at his wife and smiled. 'Of course we do. We'll direct you to it in the morning.'

Just then, there was a discreet tapping on the door and, when the weaver eased it open, they heard him having a whispered conversation with someone out on the street.

'It's about your mare,' he said, when he returned. 'She's in safe hands.' Sitting down beside them again, he explained, 'When the militia left the Brazen Head to go after the two of you, one of our men collected her and now she's up here. She's in a stable not far away.'

Tom thanked him profusely, adding, 'The soldiers were very quick off their mark.'

The weaver laughed. 'Well, the Dublin Militia may not know much about the country, but they know a cart-horse when they see one.'

The all laughed at that, and Antrim John asked, 'But will that not cause a problem for us tomorrow?'

'Well,' said the weaver, 'the problem is she's not the sort of horse you'd expect to see a saddle on. But we'll think of something.'

Soon they stopped talking and began to eat. As they did so, Tom remembered the sort of sweet smell they had got after leaving the stench of the Liffey.

'It's probably the smell from Guinness's brewery,' the woman told him. 'But, you know, we've been living here so long we don't even notice it.'

'Well, it's nice, whatever it is,' said Tom. 'It made me feel hungry.'

Antrim John laughed. 'Now that I know what it is, it'll make me feel thirsty.'

○ But for the fact that I was greatly fatigued, Tom wrote in his journal, I would not have slept a wink that night. Our weaver and his wife gave us the comfort of the loft above their loom. At the same time, their account of the activities of Major Sirr and his men had filled both

Antrim John and myself with a great sense of unease. It was a feeling that was not helped by the knowledge that we were so close to Dublin Castle which we knew to be the source of power in our unfortunate country. Fears that Major Sirr might burst into the house and arrest us contrived to keep me awake. However, as I have already pointed out, I was greatly fatigued from the exertions of our journey from Meath, and I am happy to record that my fatigue soon overcame my fears, though not without a struggle.

Dublin, I found, was a busy place. When we ventured out next morning I saw that the streets were full of traffic. People of all ages were coming and going, although where they were coming from or going to, I couldn't imagine. The horses, I noticed, were well shod so as to get a grip on the cobble-stones and they needed all the strength they could muster to pull their carts as some of the streets were very steep.

To my delight I found that our friends had brought Betsy up from the Brazen Head and had yoked her up to a cart. As we climbed aboard, the weaver told us that if we were stopped our driver would say we were going to collect a load of turf.

'This way you won't arouse any suspicions,' said the weaver. 'Leave the talking to the driver. I'll join you when we get clear of the city and give you all the directions you need.'

We thanked the weaver and his wife for all their kindness and soon we were swept out into the flow of the great metropolis. Soldiers in uniforms of all colours and descriptions patrolled the streets, some on foot, others on horseback, but they paid not the slightest attention to the turfcutter's cart. Perhaps they were looking for a man and a boy, and a carthorse with a saddle, but if they were, they were disappointed. Betsy was 'hidden' between the shafts of our cart and her saddle was on a lighter horse that followed. The weaver was in the saddle, and he was keeping an eye on us from a discreet distance.

After a while our driver told us that we were approaching Harold's Cross where Colonel Joe had had to hide to escape from the soldiers. The driver explained that we would have to cross the Grand Canal before we were in the clear. The military, we were told, were making great use of the canal. They moved troops by barge and, where the canal circled around the south side of the city, it was used as a line of defence with the soldiers guarding the bridges.

How Colonel Joe had managed to get past the soldiers on the canal, I do not know, but our story that we were going to collect a load of turf was accepted without question and we were waved through. Ahead of us we could see a line of trees and, in the distance beyond them, the mountains. As the soldiers were left farther and farther behind, we felt much safer, but it wasn't until we reached the trees that the driver pulled up and dismounted. It was now safe, he told us, to take the horse and continue on our own. Elated with the thought that we had escaped from the city we immediately jumped from the cart and helped him to unfasten the harness.

Looking back, we were delighted to see that the weaver wasn't far behind. Our delight, however, was short-lived. Almost immediately, a group of soldiers emerged on to the road behind him and, suspecting that we were up to something, they shouted to us not to move. By this time, however, we had unhitched Betsy. Antrim John immediately swung up on her back, pulled me up behind him and off we galloped. As we did so, a shot rang out and I heard the musket-ball whizzing over our heads. We ducked, but kept going.

Behind us we could hear the driver shouting to the soldiers, by way of excuse, that we had stolen his horse. Fortunately, there were no more shots, for the weaver shouted, 'I'll get them,' and galloped after us. We couldn't see him, but we knew he was coming and was in between us and the soldiers.

When we reckoned it was safe we slowed down and the weaver joined us. He was laughing at the good of it all and we laughed too, although, to be truthful, ours was a false kind of laughter, brought on, I imagine, by the narrowness of our escape. Nevertheless, we were grateful once again to our weaver who had imparted not only hospitality to us, but protection, yet never his name.

We transferred the saddle to Betsy and as we walked on the weaver pointed ahead, saying, 'That's the Dublin Mountains.'

'You said you knew where the Enchanted House was,' I reminded him.

'So I did,' he said, and pointing to the mountains again, told us, 'That's it – up there.'

'You mean, that house on top of the mountain?' asked Antrim John.

The weaver smiled at us and nodded. 'That's it. The Enchanted House. Once you get there you'll be safe. Wicklow's just on the other side of it.' O

The Enchanted House

Even before he had left his home in Newbridge, Tom had been aware that the Society of United Irishmen was a secret one and that its members used secret handshakes and other signals to identify one another. At one stage, he has heard his mother speak of these things as silly, even childish. Needless to say, such things as secret handshakes had appealed to him and his young friends and they had invented their own. It was all a game, or so they thought, but now he knew better. Had it not been for the secret signals, Antrim John and he would never have found their supporters in Dublin. They would never have made their way through the city without these people and they would never have found the Enchanted House.

Following the weaver's directions, they kept going until they came to the River Dodder and turned right. If they followed the river back up towards its source, the weaver had told them, they would find their way to Mount Pelier, on the summit of which was the Enchanted House. If they had any difficulty, he had added in parting, they should make their way to the Valley of the Thrushes. It was only when they inquired further for directions that they discovered that the weaver had been using secret names for these places, names those outside the society, including the military, were probably unaware of. Nonetheless, the weaver had shown them the Enchanted House, and all they had to do was try and keep it in sight.

'I hope he got back in to the Liberties safely,' said Tom.

They were both walking along the river now, giving Betsy a rest before they started the climb.

'Oh, don't worry about him,' replied Antrim John.' He knows what he's doing. His plan was to yoke his own horse up to the cart and drive back in with it. It was a good plan, wasn't it?'

Tom smiled. 'It sure was. I wonder what his name was?'

Antrim John shook his head. 'Who knows? But then, as I said before, the less names we know the better.'

After a while they crossed the river and, as they drew closer to Mount Pelier, the house on top gradually disappeared from view. However, they knew in their minds' eye where it was and, after a long arduous climb, they reached the top. Not quite knowing what to expect, they emerged from the trees and there, on the bare summit, was the building that Colonel Holt had called the Enchanted House.

It was, they could see, a two-storey building made entirely of stone. Even the roof was made of stones and tufts of grass were growing here and there between them. Wondering if it was occupied, they walked cautiously around it. It was built in the shape of a cross, and they began to wonder if, perhaps, it was some kind of church. Then they realised that it was a ruin. Venturing inside, they saw that the ceilings of the rooms were also made of stone and were arched. Upstairs they found a fire-place, but knew that if they lit a fire the smoke would be seen for miles around.

Standing on the wide sill of one of the front windows, Tom could see the whole of Dublin spread before him. 'Look at the view,' he said. 'And there's Dublin bay. It's as blue as the sky. And look at all the sailing ships!'

Antrim John was beside him now. 'Aye, it's a fine view, Tom boy. A fine view.'

'And look, over there to the left,' said Tom. 'I'm sure that's Meath, away there on the horizon.'

'Aye. It reminds me of the day we stood at Carbury Castle.'

'And you said you could see all the way to Antrim, remember?'

Antrim John laughed. 'Deed I do. Now, I wonder if we can see Wicklow from here?'

Tom followed him to a window at the back, only to find that their view was blocked by trees.

The sun was going down now, but it was still warm, so they sat down on the grass outside and wondered what they should do.

'I don't know about you, Tom boy,' said Antrim John, 'but I'm tired. I think we should rest here for the night and then, tomorrow, hopefully we can make it back to Whelp Rock.'

'I'm tired myself,' Tom confessed. 'And so's Betsy. I thought for a while there she was beginning to limp.'

Betsy was grazing quietly a short distance away and, looking across at her, Antrim John remarked, 'Did you? I didn't notice anything wrong with her.'

'She seems to be all right now,' said Tom.

As they talked, Tom wondered if Colonel Holt had spent a night in the Enchanted House.

'More than likely,' said Antrim John. 'And if I know him, he's at Whelp Rock now, gathering another army around him.'

'I wonder if many others have passed through here on the way back from Meath?'

'I'm sure they have – if they were lucky enough to escape the military.'

'And what will happen the ones that were caught?'

'If they're not hanged, they'll probably end up on one of those ships down there in the bay.'

'You mean, they're prison ships?' asked Tom.

Antrim John nodded. 'I'd say the big ones are all right.'

'Why do they transport people to other countries?' asked Tom. 'Why don't they just put them in jail?'

'Because the jails are full. Anyway, I suppose they reckon that if they're in a faraway country they won't be causing any more trouble here.'

Lying back on the grass, Tom closed his eyes and

thought of all the things that had happened since the day they had set out from Whelp Rock to march on Clonard. 'What was it all about, John?' he asked.

'What was all about?'

Tom sat up again. 'All the marching, all the fighting, all the dying. What was it all for?'

'Sometimes I wonder myself,' said Antrim John. 'And when I do, three words keep coming into my mind – liberty equality, fraternity. The French used them during their revolution, and we borrowed them.'

'But what do they mean?'

'Well, at first, it meant that we all wanted to be treated equally – no matter what our religion. But it was more than that. We also wanted a bit more independence for our Parliament. After that, I suppose one thing led to another, and we wanted our liberty.'

'You never told me what religion you were,' said Tom.

'That's right. I never did. I'm just an Antrim man and that's the way I want it to be.'

'How do you mean?'

'Well, some day I want to see us all living together, not wanting to know what religion the other man is, but respecting his right to have whatever religion he chooses. Politics too. I suppose I'm talking about the right of every man to take whatever path in life he wants to take.'

'But you chose to join the Antrim Militia,' Tom reminded him.

'So I did, and so did many others. I suppose it was a job. Some of us were already members of the United Irishmen, but whether we were or not, a lot of us were waiting to see how things would go. Then some cruel things happened, things that helped us to make up our minds.'

'And what made up your mind?'

Before Antrim John could answer, a large grey dog emerged from the trees and bounded towards them. It was an ugly-looking dog of indeterminate breed and it snarled and bared its teeth as it ran. Frightened, they jumped to their feet and were about to take to their heels when a voice called the dog back. At the same time they saw a man running forward to catch the dog and pull it back by the scruff of the neck. 'It's all right,' the man told them, 'he won't harm you.'

Studying the man as he approached, Tom could see that he was tall and robust, with a long straggly head of hair and a beard. He carried a hefty hazel-stick in one hand and walked in a way that suggested he was no stranger to the mountains. Putting his stick under his arm, he shook hands with Antrim John and Tom knew immediately, from the way his friend relaxed, that a signal had been passed between them.

The stranger seated himself in the grass and the dog lay down beside him. Pointing his stick in the general direction of the area that lay beyond Dublin, he said, 'I take it you've come from Meath?'

Antrim John sat down beside him, saying, 'Aye, that we have.'

'You wouldn't be heading for Whelp Rock by any chance?'

Antrim John, who was looking straight ahead, replied, 'We might.'

The stranger nodded. 'I met a man who passed through here, must have been the night before last. Said he was going to Whelp Rock. Asked me to keep an eye out for a young boy riding a cart-horse. Said he might be with a big man with a northern accent.'

Tom smiled. 'We've been trying to catch up with him.'

The man got up to go. 'You'll be spending the night here then?' When they nodded, he added, 'I'll bring you some food and blankets.'

When the stranger had gone, Tom asked, 'What do you think? Is he all right?'

'Well,' said Antrim John, 'he responded to my signal. More than that I cannot say.'

Encounter at the Hell Fire Club

CITY OF LIMERICK
CIVIC LIBRARY

It was almost dark now, but instead of retiring to the house, Antrim John suggested that they should wait in the trees in case the stranger returned with soldiers. Within an hour, however, the big dog found them and they were relieved to discover its master had returned, not with soldiers, but with the food and blankets he had promised.

As darkness closed in around them, lights began to twinkle in the city below, and as the three sat on the grass they ate and talked some more.

'What was this place?' asked Tom. 'A church?'

The stranger laughed. 'Far from it.'

'But our friend called it the Enchanted House,' said Tom.

'And with good reason,' said the stranger. 'Up here we call it the Hell Fire Club.'

'How come?' asked Antrim John.

'Well, it was built as a hunting-lodge almost eighty years ago for Thomas Conolly, Speaker of the House of Commons. But he did a thing local people never approved of. He used the stones from an ancient cairn that stood here on the hill. Shortly afterwards, there was a storm and the slated roof was blown off. It was a very violent storm and locals believed that the roof had been blown off by the devil because the cairn had been desecrated.'

'Is that why why they call it the Hell Fire Club?' asked Tom.

The man shook his head and the dog lowered its nose on to its forepaws, almost as if it knew what he was going to say. 'No. There was worse to come. Not to be out-done, Mr Conolly built a new roof on it, this time of stone, keying the stones together the way you would do in the arches of a bridge. Oh, it was a grand house, by all accounts. It had a parlour, drawing-room, kitchen, servants' quarters, everything. Then, about thirty years ago a strange group of people began to meet in it. They called themselves the Hell Fire Club. They met in secret but there were reports of debauchery, gambling and excessive drinking. Worst of all, they were said to practise Satanism.'

'What's that?' asked Tom.

'Devil worship,' the stranger told him. 'It was said they kept a black cat as Satan's representative and there were rumours of black masses being celebrated.'

'How did people know that?' asked Antrim John. 'I mean, if they were meeting in secret.'

Tom swallowed hard. Suddenly he felt cold and put his hands between his knees to keep them warm.

'Well, it came about this way,' the stranger continued. 'One night, they say, a young clergyman was crossing the mountains when there was a snowstorm. Seeing the building, he thought it was a farmhouse, but when he sought refuge in it, he found the club members having a meal.'

'And what was wrong with that?' asked Tom.

'Nothing,' said the stranger. 'But what did he see sitting at the top of the table but a black cat. He was told it was Satan's representative. So he tried to exorcise it, you know, drive the devil out of it. But the cat cried out in pain and jumped up on to a chandelier. The chandelier fell, setting the building on fire.'

There was a silence for a moment, and Antrim John said, 'So that's why they called it the Hell Fire Club.'

The man nodded, and Tom asked, 'Do you believe it? I mean, the bit about the devil and the black cat?'

The stranger got up to go and the dog got up too. 'Well, it's there and it's a ruin, so some of it must be true.'

'We were told that if we had any problem we should make our way to the valley of the Thrushes,' said Antrim John.

'The Valley of the Thrushes?' the man repeated. 'That's a secret Valley You'd never find it on your own. Anyway, you've no need to go there. Your friend has gone to Whelp Rock. You should find him there.'

The Prodigal Son

O The stranger, Tom recorded in his journal, was obviously reluctant to tell us more about the Valley of the Thrushes and it was only later that we learned why. After spending the night at the Enchanted House, Colonel Joe had gone down the mountain to make contact with his long-suffering wife, Hester, and their children. They were, at that stage, hiding in a secluded valley called Glenasmole and, to protect them, it was referred to only by what it meant in Gaelic – the Valley of the Thrushes.

The less we knew about the Valley of the Thrushes, therefore, the better and, even though we were puzzled at the time, we respected the man's decision not to tell us about it. If only he had been as circumspect when we asked him about the Enchanted House. After hearing about the black cat and the devil worship that had gone on there, Antrim John and I were of the same mind. We wrapped ourselves up in the blankets and stayed where we were – out in the open where we were safe. Even then, I prayed to the Almighty to keep me safe and, whatever faith my big friend from Antrim belonged to, it mattered not a whit. I snuggled in close to him and was glad once more of his protection.

When morning came we again admired the view of the city that lay before us. Then, with a last look back at the Enchanted House, we collected Betsy and headed for Whelp Rock. As we crossed the mountains we were sustained by the remainder of the food that the stranger had brought us, and supplemented it by eating fraughans, a word, I discovered, that Antrim John had not heard before. Nor was he familiar with the blue berries, but he helped me to pick them and agreed that they were quite succulent.

By this time, Betsy had become lame and we were forced to walk slowly with her, stopping often to let her rest. Eventually, however, we arrived at Whelp Rock, where we were given a warm reception and furnished with refreshments. Colonel Joe, we were told, had gone on to Glenmalure where large numbers of survivors from Clonard had gathered, including many of the wounded.

I was, of course, anxious to return to my home but I could not do so without Betsy. Antrim John, on the other hand, was anxious to join Colonel Joe but, loyal as always, he vowed he would not leave me until Betsy was better.

And so we whiled away the remaining days of July at Whelp Rock. Each day seemed to bring new strength to Betsy and soon she was ready to resume the journey. I thought I would never see Colonel Joe again, but I should have known better. As we were about to leave, the word went up that a large body of rebels was approaching from the direction of Glenmalure. And riding at the head of them was none other than Colonel Joe. Somehow he had managed to band together almost a thousand men. He had been elected their commander-in-chief, was now a general, and was continuing the campaign, confident that the French would honour their promise to render assistance.

Among General Joe's new force, we discovered, were members of various militias, including more than two dozen of Antrim's John's former colleagues who had left the Antrim Militia in Arklow. Shortly after the rebels pitched camp, we saw the hooded figure of the Moving Magazine walking among them once more, distributing musket-balls, powder and, I have no doubt, information.

When we went to see General Joe we also discovered that he was being attended by a new *aide-de-camp* – Croppy Biddy. She was dressed in a green habit, a kind of uniform with epaulets, and was known as the General's Lady. She seemed to be a determined rebel and appeared highly gratified with her distinction.

As General Joe rode away, he smiled at me and, when I looked at his high brow, his short, black, receding hair and the beard under his chin, I couldn't help but wonder once again if my mother would regard him as handsome. Somehow, I thought she would.

With the new rebel army went my friend and protector, Antrim John. I was saddened to see him go, but I was anxious to return to my family. So I saddled Betsy and we made our way back down into the Avoca valley.

All the time I was away my parents had no way of knowing whether I was alive or dead and it was with much rejoicing that they received me back into our home. Thereafter my father abandoned his Sunday readings from Revelations. Instead, he would open the family Bible at the Gospel According to St Luke and read about the return of the prodigal son. O

Aftermath

In late September, General Holt led his forces into Aughrim where they attacked the notorious Hunter Gowan and his men, forcing them to make an ignominious retreat from the town. At one stage thirty-nine charges of pillage and slaughter were brought against Gowan. He was arrested by the military, but on the day of the trial the prosecutor was absent – whether by accident or design isn't known – and he was discharged.

As General Holt continued his campaign, a £300 reward was offered for his capture. In October, he was suffering from wounds received when fighting his way out of an ambush. Recuperating in Dublin, he conferred with other leaders and, on 4 November, it was decided to cease hostilities. A French landing at Killala, County Mayo, had failed and there was little prospect of any further French support. Following his surrender he was transported to Australia. He returned after fifteen years and died in Kingstown (now Dun Laoghaire) in 1826.

When the rebel forces were dispersed at Longwood Bog two of the other leaders, Anthony Perry and Father Kearns, escaped but were arrested in Kings County (now Offaly), taken to Edenderry and hanged. In ill-health, the one-armed Esmond Kyan returned to Wexford where he met the same fate.

Garret Byrne continued northwards with about fifteen hundred men. After crossing the River Boyne they made a desperate stand at Knightstown Bog, beyond Navan, but were defeated, driven south and finally dispersed at Ballyboghil in north County Dublin. Byrne was allowed to go into exile in Germany, together with Edward

Fitzgerald who had discontinued the march after the battle of Clonard.

The Moving Magazine was said to be Susy O'Toole, daughter of Phelim O'Toole, a blacksmith who lived near Annamoe, County Wicklow. Although only thirty, she was able to take on the appearance of an old woman by wearing a dirty, pepper-and-salt coloured frieze cloak, adopting a stoop and dropping her jaw in such a way that changed her contenance. But, when it was necessary to act with vigour, her powerful muscles and brawny limbs were said to be more than a match for many men.

Croppy Biddy, far from being remembered as a determined rebel, or 'a heroine in green' as one account put it, became notorious as an informer, giving false evidence against many former rebels, including Garret Byrne's brother, William, who was convicted and executed in Wicklow town.

CITY OF LIMERICK
B 42707
PUBLIC LIBRARY

Kilcullen flag(top); Colonel Holt's flag

Historical Footnote

In his memoirs, General Holt says he knew young Howett's father for many years, that he lived near Newbridge and was a miller by trade. However, he doesn't tell us what the family's allegiance might have been. I, therefore, had to 'invent' the family and decided to portray them as Protestant middle-class people who supported the Rebellion. Yet, it may be that Mr Howlett was the same man referred to by Thomas Pakenham in his book, *The Year of Liberty*. Pakenham says that the driving force behind the United party in the borderland of Wexford and Wicklow in May 1798 was a group of Catholic farmers, traders and small businessmen, one of whom was a miller called Howlet. When Anthony Perry, 'the only Protestant seriously involved', was pitch-capped, says Pakenham, he confessed to all his seditious activities, 'including party meetings at his own barn at Inch (in north Wexford) and in Thomas Howlet's mill'.

Holt refers to Mr Howlett in his account of the attack on Hunter Gowan in late September. He had heard that Gowan and several corps of cavalry had taken up quarters in Aughrim and was on his way to 'pay my brave Hunter a visit', when he received a message that his son Joshua had been killed by yeomen. However, it turned out that because of the similarity in the names, Holt probably being pronounced Howlt, the yeomen had killed a son of Mr Howlett in the mistaken belief that he was Holt's son. 'I regretted much,' Holt wrote, 'that this boy lost his life on account of his name being supposed to be Holt … These wicked and abominable practices caused a great number to be killed on both sides without consideration, and I am sorry to say it came to my lot to witness too many scenes of it practised by both parties.'

There is some confusion as to which of Lieutenant Tyrell's three sons fired the shot which caused the first fatality at Clonard. Some accounts suggest it was his second son, Thomas. However, I have opted for the version in the genealogical history of the Tyrells supplied to me by members of the Tyrell family. This quotes Musgrave's *History of the Rebellion of 1798* as saying that the first shot was fired by the youngest son, George, aged fourteen. The pennant referred to in the story, with the name Whitechurch on it, was shown to me by Charlie Tyrell, his wife Nodlaig, and his brother Jasper when I visited them at Ballinderry, not far from Clonard. Descendants of Lieutenant Tyrell, Charlie and Jasper believe the pennant was captured from the rebels during the attack on the Sheriff's House. I am also indebted to both of them, and to their nephew Alan Cox, for providing me with extracts from the Tyrell family history, including the story of their coat of arms.

It was during a visit to the same area of County Meath that I came across the letter written by Major John Ormsby to Lord Castlereagh, in which he gave an account of the attack on a large contingent of rebels at Fox's Hill. I had been told about that battle by friends of mine, Brendan Egan and his wife Dolly, whose mother, Kathleen O'Connor, of Broadford, lives at Fox's Hill. From the top of the hill we could see the bog where the rebels had been overcome and, later, as we talked in the house, Mrs O'Connor showed me the letter which, over the years, had come into the family's possession. Subsequently, I was told that the letter may not have been published before, although I can't be certain of this. In thanking the family for all their help, I would like to express my gratitude to Mrs O'Connor for allowing me to use it.

Locating the site of the battle of Clonard provided my wife Frances and myself with a most enjoyable July outing. We were fortunate to find Josephine Donlon who knew not only where the remains of the Sherrif's House were to be found, but was most knowledgeable about the events that had happened there. She also introduced us to Peter Maguire, who lives beside the ruins of Tyrell's mill, and I am grateful to both of them for all their help. There is no trace of the old bridge over the River Boyne, but the stone from the doorway of the old inn, advertising good dry lodgings and breakfast, now stands on the lawn of John and Stella Burke's house, not far from the present bridge. My thanks to them and to Mrs Elizabeth Hickey of Skryne Castle, Tara, whom I consulted about the possible date of the inn.

The sign at the old inn

Acknowledgements

In the course of my research for this book, I received the most generous assistance from Dr Ruan O'Donnell and, in thanking him, I wish him well with his own publications: *The Rebellion in Wicklow, 1798* (Irish Academic Press); and 'Bridget "Croppy Biddy" Dolan, Wicklow's Anti-Heroine of 1798', in *The Women of '98* (Four Courts Press).

Once again, F. Glenn Thompson has been of great assistance to me and I wish him well with his illustrated history of the uniforms of the 1798 period which he had almost completed at the time of writing.

My thanks also to Gerry Lyne of the Genealogical Office in Dublin; Paul Doyle of the National Museum of Ireland; Eric McCleery of the Ulster Folk and Transport Museum; Dr. Raymond Refaussé, librarian and archivist and Heather Smith, assistant librarian, in the Church of Ireland Representative Body Library in Dublin; Joan Kavanagh, co-ordinator of the Heritage Centre in Wicklow town; Peter Moore, chairman of the Vale of Avoca Development Association; Marie Merrigan, chairperson of the association's history committee; Katie Kahn Carl; Siobhain Saunders, Guinness Ireland Group; and Helena Saunders.

Publications which have been of help to me include: *Memoirs of Joseph Holt, General of the Irish Rebels in 1798*, edited from his original manuscript by T. Crofton Croker, 1838; Sir Richard Musgrave's *Memoirs of the Irish Rebellion of 1798;* Thomas Cloney's *Personal Narrative*, for which I thank my good friend Dr Neil Murray; *The Life of Michael Dwyer* and *The Wexford Rising in 1798* by Charles Dickson, for which I thank my publisher Rena Dardis; *Exiles from Erin*, edited by Bob Reece (Gill and

Macmillan); *Arms & Armour* by Michele Byam (Dorling Kindersley, London); *Behind the Scenes* by Ernie Shepherd (Whitechurch Publications), which tells the story of the Hell Fire Club; *The Grand Canal of Ireland* by Ruth Delany; and *Balyna '80*, an annual parish magazine, for which I thank Gillian Kennedy of Offaly County Library.

Seal of the United Irishmen